Caleb laid his hand over hers.

"Let me speak first." His voice was warm and laced with excitement. "We have never had an understanding, but I think you care for me. Is that true?"

"*Jah.*"

"More than just as a friend?"

A smile twitched at the corners of her mouth. "*Jah.*"

"*Gut.* Until we figure out how to get around being from different Orders, can we just have an understanding that we want to see each other?"

Her fitful night's sleep last evening had filled her with fear of never seeing Caleb and his *kinner* again. Now as she looked out the buggy and across the street, that fear lunged at her throat. Her bishop was staring straight at her.

Caleb's request met with her approval, for sure, but given their differences and the scowl on the bishop's face, she was equally certain Bishop Yoder would not agree. But how far would he go to make her rethink her decision?

Marie E. Bast grew up on a farm in northern Illinois. In the solitude of country life, she often read or made up stories. She earned a BA, an MBA and an MA in general theology and enjoyed a career with the federal government, but characters kept whispering her name. She retired and now pursues her passion of full-time writing. Marie loves walking, golfing with her husband of twenty-seven years and baking. Visit Marie at mariebast.Blogspot.com.

Books by Marie E. Bast

Love Inspired

The Amish Baker

Visit the Author Profile page at Harlequin.com.

The Amish Baker

Marie E. Bast

HARLEQUIN® LOVE INSPIRED®

Recycling programs
for this product may
not exist in your area.

 LOVE INSPIRED BOOKS

ISBN-13: 978-1-335-53904-5

The Amish Baker

Copyright © 2019 by Marie Elizabeth Bast

www.Harlequin.com

Printed in U.S.A.

For I know the thoughts that I think toward you,
saith the Lord, thoughts of peace,
and not of evil, to give you an expected end.
—*Jeremiah* 29:11

My husband and sons,
you three are the joy of my life.

In loving memory of Lois Walline, my mom,
and Blanche Browning, my aunt,
the two best cooks and bakers I have ever
known. I miss you dearly.

Also, to Melissa, my editor and wizard in
disguise, for believing in me, and Scribes202,
my critique partners.

Chapter One

Sarah Gingerich stomped into her Amish Sweet Delights bakery an hour earlier than her usual arrival time of 4:00 a.m. Who could sleep a wink after what Bishop Yoder had said to her yesterday? She slid the dead bolt closed. *He had his nerve.*

Straightening her shoulders, she shook off the indignant words. *Gelassenheit*—calm down and let it go.

She scooted to the pantry for flour, mixed the bread dough, tossed it on a floured board and began kneading. After folding the soft mass over, she floured and kneaded again.

As she punched the dough a little harder than necessary, the bishop's words came rushing back to her. Heat rose from her neck to her ears, burning her now as it had when he had said them. She couldn't believe that during his preaching on the rewards of being a wife and mother, he had stared straight at her the entire time. Later, he called her aside and mentioned it was time she stopped mourning Samuel and remarried. Why would he say such a thing?

Maybe it was just a casual comment, or maybe the bishop thought he was looking out for her best interest. That's all. She steered her hands back to kneading and mentally put a circle around her bad thoughts and tossed them away.

Tears pressed at the corners of her eyes. They caught on her lashes, and she batted them away. She had her *daed*'s bakery and the apartment upstairs; she didn't need an *ehemann* for support. Sarah plopped the dough in a bowl, covered it and pushed it to the side. Then she grabbed more ingredients, stirred up several batches of yeast rolls and set them to rise.

While the yeast worked, she stirred up a spice cake and shoved it into the oven. When the cake tested done, she pulled it out and popped the bread and rolls in to bake. She set the timer and started on the pies and cookies.

When the first batch of baked goods had cooled, she carted the pastries to the front of the shop and placed them in the display case. A job Hannah Ropp, her friend and assistant, usually performed. Hannah loved to decorate the shelves with rows of cookies and cupcakes in cute patterns—maybe in a heart shape.

Where is Hannah? She's usually here by now.

Sarah set the goodies the *kinner* liked on the bottom shelf. Treats adults normally selected took over the middle shelf. The best sellers, breads and rolls claimed the prize spot on the top shelf.

Without Hannah, she didn't have time to arrange the shelves neatly. Her eyes roamed over the display. Not as *gut* a job as her friend would have done, but good enough for now.

The bakery's cell phone, which the *Ordnung* allowed for business, jingled and lit up with Hannah's name. She touched the screen. "Where are you?"

"I figured you'd forget. I have a doctor's appointment this morning and will be in around noon."

"I'm sorry. I did forget." Tension laced her voice.

"Oh, no. Is something wrong?"

"I wanted to tell you what Bishop Yoder said to me yesterday."

"What did he say?" Hannah asked, her voice steeped in concern.

"He told me it's time to get remarried." Sarah blurted into the phone. "I'm happy. I don't want an *ehemann*."

"*Ach!* I told you that I heard the bishop had a habit of pressuring some of the widows into re-marrying. Now do you believe me?"

"Hannah, that's gossiping and a sin." Sarah shook her head.

"It's only a sin if it's not true. This is true."

"Shame on you, Hannah Ropp. You're looking for loopholes in the Bible."

"*Jah, jah.* Gotta go. Hang on 'til I get there, and we'll talk about it."

"Don't hurry. I'm managing." Sarah hit the end button.

She grabbed a wet dishcloth and started wiping off the crumbs she'd spilled on the counter. As her hand zipped across the Formica, it bumped the walnut papa and mama bears Samuel had carved, knocking them over with a bang. Sarah jerked her hand back.

Slowly, she picked each one up—holding her breath—and surveyed for damage before setting it upright. She heaved a long sigh.

Both fine.

The bears were one of the few things she had left to remind her of Samuel. They brought her comfort and served as a good form of advertise-ment for the Amish artisans in the area. Many *Englischers* had admired the walnut carvings and asked for directions to the woodcraft shop.

The bishop's words flitted through her mind

again. Working fourteen hours a day in the bakery gave her little time to care for a family. Would an *ehemann* allow her to keep the shop? The bakery was her life. It was all she had. She couldn't give it up. Not to mention, she had an obligation to the town—Kalona—and to her customers.

When Samuel had died three years ago, she had stumbled through those first few weeks as if she were groping her way around a dark house without a lantern. Nothing made sense, she couldn't make a decision and she had no desire to bake. She had promised to *liebe*, honor and cherish Samuel "'til death do us part," but she'd figured that meant after fifty years of marriage and seven *kinner*.

Her heart had shattered as if it were a crystal dropped upon the floor. Hannah had helped her plow through the sorrow of Samuel's death.

But life had had no meaning after Samuel died until she returned to the bakery and continued with her cookbook that she would dedicate to her parents and the bakery they loved. Some of their recipes mingled in with her recipes.

Nein. She couldn't give up the bakery. She wouldn't. The bishop couldn't make her remarry.
Could he?

She didn't believe Hannah's gossip. Surely the bishop was only matchmaking those who wanted a spouse.

After grabbing a set of pot holders, she opened the oven door to a steamy whiff of white bread, mingled with the aroma of fresh cinnamon rolls and buttered buns. She set the pans on racks to cool. Pivoting, she glanced at the clock.

Ach. Almost time to unlock the front door.

Sarah pulled out the medium-roast and the decaf beans and started the coffee. While it brewed, she wrote the daily special on the chalk-board, then scooted to the front door, pulled the dead bolt back and flipped the sign to Open.

She puttered around the shop, setting out foam cups and filling the napkin holders. When the doorbell jingled, she stashed the napkin bags behind the counter and looked up into the face of an Amish man she'd never seen before. Judging from his trimmed beard and hair, he was New Order Amish. In her Old Order community, men didn't trim their beards.

"Welkum." Sarah whisked out her best smile.

"Danki." His voice was as quiet as his footfalls. Glancing at the pastries, he smiled and shook his head as if the decision were too much for this early in the morning.

"Can I help you?" Sarah's gaze locked with his sage-green eyes, which were set against sun-bronzed skin. A handsome face for sure and for certain. *Ach.* She stared. He'd think her a forward woman. Her cheeks heated like roasting marshmallows and she glanced away.

He removed his straw hat and twirled it around in his hands as he studied the rolls, cookies and pies. Each received a generous amount of time.

"*Gut morgen.* I'm Caleb Brenneman. How do you do?"

Sarah's stomach tickled as he looked at her. "Fine, *danki.* I'm Sarah Gingerich. I own the bakery."

"Nice to meet you. I'll have a cinnamon roll and a cup of that *gut*-smelling coffee."

She handed him the roll and coffee, then gestured to the five tables and chairs by the windows. "Feel free to have a seat."

After serving the others who'd trailed into the bakery behind Caleb, Sarah refilled the display case but sensed the newcomer's eyes watching her work. Did he know her? She couldn't place him. Because of the bakery, she was acquainted with most of the Plain community around Kalona, at least by sight. Still, the Amish were scattered in seven counties in Iowa, so there were plenty she hadn't met.

She glanced his way at the exact moment when he looked at her. *Ach–caught!* A smile brewed deep in her chest and crept onto her lips. "Do you live around here, Caleb?"

"I bought a farm north of town."

"You're from Iowa then?"

"I grew up here. When I met my *frau*, I moved to Seymour, Missouri. After Martha got cancer, I moved her and our family back, so she could have treatment in Iowa City, and we'd be closer to my *bruder* Peter and his family."

The doorbell jingled and Sarah reluctantly peeled her eyes away from Caleb and focused on her customer. "*Gut* mornin'."

"Morning, Sarah." Mrs. Wallin smiled as she entered the bakery. "Just a loaf of white bread today."

Caleb finished his cinnamon roll and coffee, tossed his cup in the wastebasket next to the counter and tipped his hat to Sarah. "Have a *gut* day."

Sarah gave a nod. "You, too." As she was bagging the white bread for Mrs. Wallin, she peered up and caught his wink, and had to steady her hands.

Her pulse jumped. Her mind raced in a hundred different directions, but only for a few seconds. What was she thinking? She didn't want to remarry. The bakery was her life.

Caleb strode toward his buggy, his heart pounding like a blacksmith's hammer. Sarah's chocolate-brown hair and cinnamon-brown eyes had stolen his attention. He'd tried to refocus but couldn't keep his eyes from following her. He could have sat in the bakery all day, staring at her as she worked.

Still, it was unmistakable with her navy blue dress and the shape of her prayer *kapp*. She was Old Order Amish. If she were single, where could the relationship go? He enjoyed the liberties his church allowed—shorter beard and hair, Sunday school and Bible study. The Old Order wanted only the church to interpret Scriptures, while New Order encouraged small group study.

His church even believed in church outreach and helping the non-Amish. They also permitted electric conveniences, such as the tractor, mechanical milker and refrigerator, rototiller, lawn mower, chainsaw and propane gas. Without grown *sohns* to help Caleb, he needed such things on the farm.

He must chase thoughts of the beautiful baker out of his head. A relationship between Old Order and New Order would never work. *Jah*, he must forget about Sarah with the cinnamon-brown eyes and concentrate on his farming and crops.

Caleb climbed into his buggy and tapped the leather straps against Snowball's back. "Giddyap, slowpoke. I have chores waiting at home."

As the horse trotted along, Caleb gawked at his neighbors' fields and mentally compared theirs to his. *Jah*, his looked *gut*, maybe better.

Caleb parked the buggy by the barn, stepped down and welcomed the cool breeze that swept across his face. He pulled his hat off, swiped a hand over his brow and then plopped his hat back on his head.

His mind steered his hands back to the job at hand. As he unhitched the horse and walked him to his stall, Caleb tried to push Sarah's image from his head. What was wrong with him? He was acting like a sixteen-year-old *bu* who was getting ready to court.

This was nonsense. Martha had died only a year ago; it wasn't time to start thinking about getting another *frau*.

Nein. Nein. Too soon.

Sarah glanced up as Melinda Miller maneuvered her shopping bags through the bakery doorway. "Congratulations on your *sohn*. I have a *boppli* gift for little Abraham's *mamm* and *daed* to enjoy." Sarah scooted to the kitchen, snatched the gift box off a table, returned to the front and handed the box to the new *mamm*. "I was going to drop it by after work today, but you saved me the trip."

Melinda lifted the cover enough to peek in. "It's a cookie shaped like a little buggy with a *boppli* in it. It looks delicious. *Danki*, Sarah." She leaned over the counter, her face beaming like that of a five-year-old girl with a new dress. "A dozen maple-pecan rolls. Motherhood is *wunderbaar.* Too bad you and Samuel never had *kinner.*"

The words slammed into Sarah, wrapped around her scarred heart and squeezed. She and Samuel had wanted a *kind*, a child. Concealing the ache in her chest with a smile barely there, she worked swiftly to bag the order and hand it to Melinda. She took the money, slipped it into the drawer and then slumped a hip against the counter to help ease the pain.

"*Danki*, Sarah. I'll see you next week." Melinda opened the door carefully, trying not to bump her baked goods while guiding her shopping bags.

Alvin Studer held the door for Melinda. When she was through, he entered.

He walked by the display case, slowly checking out the sweets. "You're a *gut* cook, Sarah."

"*Danki*, Alvin, but you mean baker."

"What?" He looked up, his eyes full of puzzlement.

"Never mind." She waited for his order as he paced the floor, looking at breads and rolls, then stealing glances at her. He bent his tall, lanky frame closer to the display case and peered inside. His long face twisted with indecision.

Sarah's mind wandered back to Caleb Brenneman. Remembering his handsome face pulled a smile across her mouth as she fought to push it away. Most Amish men didn't come into the bakery, so she'd probably never see him again. That was *gut*—she'd forget about him in a few days.

"Have you made a selection yet, Alvin?"

He stepped to the counter and gave her a smile while his eyes roved over her. "A loaf of cinnamon-raisin bread." He hesitated. "Would you like to go for a buggy ride with me Saturday night, Sarah?"

Stunned, she stepped back. She didn't want to go for a ride with Alvin, or any other man. She had her life. It was comfortable, and she liked things as they were. But with Alvin, she'd heard he had hit his last *frau*, so the answer was an emphatic *nein*. Yet the idea of courting anyone who wasn't Samuel frightened her.

How should she answer Alvin? She hated to be rude, though she wanted no misunderstanding in how she felt. "*Danki*, Alvin, but my shop requires all my time. When I'm not out front, I'm in the back, baking. I have no free time to squeeze in a buggy ride. Sorry, but that's the life of a baker."

His eyes turned dark and mean. His expression hinted that he wanted to say something but didn't.

She drew in a ragged breath. Her hands fumbled as she plucked the bread from the shelf, almost dropping it. She shoved the loaf in a sack and set it on the counter. "*Danki*, Alvin."

He stared at her. The doorbell jingled twice as the stout Bertha Bontrager bumped the door with her hip as she entered. Alvin didn't flinch at the noise.

Sarah blew out the breath she was holding. "Afternoon, Bertha. What can I do for you today?"

"The bishop said you'd be receptive to my invitation," Alvin whispered as he tossed Sarah a cold look and laid a five-dollar bill on the counter. "Keep the change. I'll see you next time." He grabbed his sack and stomped out the door.

Sarah was stunned and winced as a shiver ran up her spine.

Sarah took advantage of the lull in business after the lunch hour and wiped down the counter. The door opened and Hannah whooshed in like a butterfly.

"*Hullo.* Sorry I'm late. My appointment took longer than I thought it would."

"Don't worry. I managed just fine."

Hannah hurried to the sink and washed her hands while Sarah loaded a tray with cookies. "Have you baked the afternoon order yet?"

"*Nein.* I've been too busy."

Hannah disappeared through the kitchen doorway. "I'll start it."

After the bell tinkled, a cool breeze swept over Sarah. She glanced up from cleaning the display case and froze as Bishop Yoder approached the counter.

"Do you have a cup of coffee and a slice of banana bread left? I'd like to sit and rest a spell."

"*Jah*, but it's the last cup of coffee in the pot so it's free. Sit. I'll bring it to the table."

Her stomach roiled at the bishop's presence. She poured the strong brew and laid a slice of banana bread on a plate. She drew a deep breath. He very seldom came into her bakery. His *frau* was one of the best cooks in the community. She carried a tray with his coffee and banana bread to the table and set it down in front of him. "Enjoy, Bishop Yoder."

"*Danki*, Sarah. Please sit and join me."

Her feet itched to move away. "Only for a minute—I have to start cleaning the display case for closing."

"This will only take a minute." He took a bite of the banana bread, then a sip of coffee. "This bread is very *gut*."

She pulled a wooden chair away from the table and sat.

"I believe Alvin Studer came into the bakery and asked you to join him for a buggy ride. He is a *gut* man and his six *kinner* need a *mamm*."

A shiver ran up her spine as she averted her eyes from the bishop's face. "*Jah*. He did ask. I

was busy and didn't have time to talk with him."
It was only a little white lie.

"Sarah, it's *Gott*'s will that you remarry. Each
person in our church must lose the desire for self
and think of the community. That is what we believe. *Jah*, it's time for you to sell the bakery. It's
Satan's lie that makes you think that a career outside the home is fulfilling. Alvin needs a *frau* and
mamm for his *kinner*." His eyes pierced hers like
the tiny, sharp point on a straight pin.

The bishop was matchmaking her!

Chapter Two

Plop...plop.

Caleb stopped and listened.

Plop. The sound cut through the still afternoon. He turned his head in the direction of the pond but couldn't see past the grove of maple trees. Maybe an animal skittered over the water. He trained his concentration back to the job at hand.

Plop...plop.

Caleb listened. *Jah*, definitely coming from the pond. Surely Jacob hadn't skipped school again to go fishing.

He laid his fence-mending tools on the ground and raced across the field. His long strides carried him quickly to the shade of the trees. Scanning the perimeter of the pond, his eyes came to rest on his six-year-old *sohn* reclining on the grass.

Caleb walked to within ten feet of the *bu*. "Jacob, what are you doing?"

Jacob sprang to his feet, almost losing his balance as he teetered on the edge of the pond. He stepped back and whirled around. "I'm th-throwing r-rocks in the water." His head hung, but his brooding gray eyes peered up.

"Again, you skipped school. Are your chores done?" Caleb's intent gaze froze Jacob to the spot.

Jacob shrugged his shoulders. *"Nein."*

"Work on the farm takes priority over playing." Caleb furrowed his brow. "You know chores always come first. Milk cows need to maintain a strict schedule."

"I-I'm sorry," Jacob whispered, almost too low for Caleb to hear.

"What has gotten into you?"

Jacob shrugged again with a blank face.

"Go and unhook the gate and let it swing open so the cows can come in from the pasture for milking. Then feed the chickens. After chores, go to the house and get on your knees and ask *Gott* to forgive your laziness." Caleb turned and walked back to the fence but glanced over his shoulder to make sure Jacob headed toward the barnyard. Caleb shook his head as he watched the *bu* kick a stone in his path.

"Jacob, don't take your anger out on the earth. Anger is a sinful thing. In prayer today, tell the Lord your transgression. Go, sit in silence and talk to Him about what you have done. We'll discuss an extra chore for your punishment."

Caleb watched as Jacob trudged to the barn-yard with his shoulders slumped. He would leave the *bu* alone for a while to think about what he'd done.

His wife's death had been hardest on his *sohn*. Jacob had cried for hours after the cancer took his *mamm*. Martha's caring ways had woven a strong bond between her and the *bu*.

Caleb returned to the pasture. Holding a piece of wire fencing, he stretched it tight around the wood post, pulled the hammer out of his belt and drove a staple over the wire to secure it. He walked down the fence line, found another piece of loose fencing and fixed it. Mr. Warner, on the farm next door, didn't much care for Caleb's cows trampling down his corn.

He took a step back, removed his hat and wiped trickles of perspiration from his brow while he surveyed the work. After smacking the hat against his thigh to remove dust and moisture from it, he plopped it back on.

For a small *bu*, Jacob gave Caleb more problems than this old fence. *Jacob, Jacob, Jacob, how do I get through to you?*

He looked up toward heaven. *Lord, what do I do with him?*

Caleb had consulted the bishop about Jacob's

sadness after his *mamm* had died. "Time will cover the wound," the bishop had said, "like a healing salve."

Martha had passed over a year ago, but the salve hadn't eased Jacob's pain. At least, not yet.

Like Jacob, Caleb had thought about Martha a lot at first. He'd missed her terribly. Yet ever since the encounter with the pretty baker, he couldn't erase the memory of Sarah's smile, her chocolate-brown hair or those cinnamon-brown eyes. They started pushing the memories of Martha into a secret spot in his mind. Was it right to let new memories replace those he had of Martha? He touched his hand to his stomach, where Sarah's nearness had stirred him. For sure and for certain, she was an attractive woman.

Was it too soon to remarry? Jah, his *kinner* needed a *mamm*, but a woman as nice-looking as Sarah must have an *ehemann*. Guilt prickled the back of his neck, and he shook Sarah's image from his mind.

He grabbed his fence-mending tools, carted them back to the barn and hung each one on a hook. Then he pulled off his gloves, straightened them out and laid them flat on the bench. When he walked past the milking floor, he saw that Mary had already led the Holsteins to the stanchions and had started applying the iodine mixture to the cows' udders. Jacob sat off to the side, watching and learning. Caleb smiled. In a couple of years, the *bu* could take over that chore.

It'd be nice to have his *sohn* work alongside him. Someday, Jacob would own the farm, unless Caleb remarried and had another *sohn*. Then the youngest *bu* would inherit the farm, according to Amish custom, and he'd give his older *bu*, Jacob, money to start his own business. Mary would find some young *bu* to marry, and he'd have his own farm or business to take care of Mary and their family.

Caleb followed Mary and wiped the cow's udders with an alcohol wipe. When he was finished with the disinfecting, he attached the vacuum line and started the milking process.

Glancing at Jacob sitting quietly and wearing a sorrowful face, Caleb racked his brain for a way to help the *bu* deal with grieving and his feelings of emptiness and loneliness. Sometimes he wished Jacob were more like Mary.

At thirteen, she was strong willed and self-sufficient. From an early age, Mary did for herself. Her independent way seemed to help her deal with her mother's death and grieving the loss.

Jah, for sure and for certain, *Gott* had blessed Mary with a tenacious personality and a thriving business making jellies, candies and crafts the *Englisch* liked.

Nein. Jacob wasn't as tough as Mary. He was the sensitive one.

Caleb had a surprise for Jacob tomorrow. One that just might ease his pain for at least a little while.

Caleb settled on the seat and watched his *sohn* mosey toward the buggy. Jacob climbed in and plopped down beside his *daed.* Caleb shook the reins. "Giddyap, Snowball."

"Why do we have to go to Kalona, Daed?" His lips set in a pout.

"We are going to drop off some of Mary's pillow covers, pot holders and *boppli* blankets at a consignment shop."

"Why can't Mary go instead of me?"

"She is busy with the housework, cooking, laundry and making things to sell."

"I don't want to go."

Caleb looked at the *bu* a moment, trying to figure out what would make Jacob happy. Most *kinner* would enjoy a trip to town. "You will go and help. Not another word about it."

A few minutes later, he glanced at his *sohn.* Jacob held his back straight as a stick, staring straight ahead. What could he possibly do for the *bu* to take the stiffness and hurt out of his heart?

Caleb gave up on conversation and instead rubbernecked at his neighbors' fields the whole three miles to Kalona. *Jah*, his fields looked as *gut* as these.

Their errands didn't take long, as Snowball trotted them around town. Caleb hadn't eaten much for breakfast, so a roll and cup of coffee would sure be *gut* right about now. He stopped the buggy one shop down from the bakery.

"Where are we going now?" Jacob looked from one side of the street to the other.

"You'll see. It's a surprise." Caleb walked beside Jacob and ushered him to the Amish Sweet Delights bakery, opened the door and motioned for Jacob to enter. As his *sohn* passed, Caleb detected a trace of a smile.

Caleb leaned down by Jacob's ear and whispered, "You can order anything in the case. Ask for a glass of milk, too. We'll sit a minute and refresh ourselves."

Two customers stood in front of them. The man at the counter was an *Englischer*, clean-shaven and wearing brown trousers and a matching shirt—the same kind of clothing that Caleb had seen on deliverymen. His stomach tightened as he overheard the man tell Sarah how nice she looked today.

She didn't appear to hear him. "Who's next?"

The woman in front of Caleb took her turn at the counter. The bakery door behind Caleb opened, and two young Amish *buwe*, Noah and

Matthew, entered and stood in line behind them. The *buwe* tapped Jacob on the shoulders, letting him know they were back there. They talked and laughed, trying to coax Jacob into a conversation.

The woman in front paid, picked up her sack and left.

"We're next, Jacob." Caleb stepped forward as the *buwe* joked and teased Jacob about a girl in school. He glanced back over his shoulder. "Jacob, it is our turn to order."

"*Nein*, I don't like her." Jacob spouted the words at his friend and gave Matthew a shove. Jacob whirled back around, stepped on a broken cookie or something on the floor and lunged forward. His arms flung out as he slid across the counter, hitting the walnut bears and sending them sailing through the air. They banged on a table, bounced off and smashed against the wall.

Jacob's eyes widened and his mouth gaped as he stumbled back away from the counter. Caleb caught him and steadied Jacob until he regained his balance.

Everyone at the tables stopped talking and stared at the commotion. The men at the table where the broken bears lay shoved their chairs away from the pieces.

Stunned, Caleb wasn't sure what to do. He looked from the bears to Sarah. She shrieked and ran to retrieve the fragments. Tears clouded her eyes, threatening to spill over as she hugged the pieces to her chest and walked back to the counter.

Caleb placed a hand on Jacob's shoulder. "Jacob, you have broken them."

"I'm sorry. I didn't mean to do that."

Sarah laid the pieces behind the counter, straightened and looked at Jacob. "I know you didn't. They shouldn't have sat there. It's my fault."

Caleb removed his wide-brimmed straw hat from his head. "Sarah, I can take the pieces and make you a new set. They won't match exactly, but it'll be close and most won't tell the difference."

She swallowed hard and shook her head. "No, that's not necessary. It wouldn't be quite the same. These were the last things my husband made me before he passed away." Her voice caught in her throat.

Caleb glanced over his shoulder at every pair of eyes in the bakery boring a hole through his back. His cheeks burned, and he sucked in a deep breath. "Jacob must pay for the damage he caused."

"*Nein*, Caleb, it's not necessary." She placed an index finger at the corner of her eye and blotted a tear that had escaped.

"Jacob will be here early Saturday morning to help you in the shop. He can clean the tables, the chairs and the floor, and help fetch supplies. Whatever you need him to do, for as long as you need him, until he pays off the debt. He must make amends."

Sarah looked at Jacob, a small-framed *bu*, maybe six or seven years old, with a tuft of blond hair poking out from under his hat. "Do you want to help me?" she asked, softening her voice.

He nodded. His sulking brown eyes resembled those of a scolded puppy and tugged at the edges of her heart.

"*Gut.* I'd appreciate that." She let a smile pluck at the corners of her mouth.

"We'll take three cinnamon rolls to go, please." Caleb plopped his hat on his head. "Again, we are very sorry." The red flush in his cheeks deepened, but Sarah pretended not to notice.

Sarah handed the order to him over the counter. Caleb's hand glided over hers as he grasped the sack, sending an unexpected rush through her. The warmth jabbed at her heart as though a tiny arrow had pierced it. She jerked back in response. She hadn't felt the touch of a man's hand in a long time.

The sensation had startled her. Or maybe it was her reaction that had startled her.

She'd enjoy getting to know Jacob and most assuredly his papa, too.

Chapter Three

The scent of lilacs and freshly cut grass saturated the morning breeze. Caleb inhaled a deep whiff and watched as Jacob climbed into the buggy and sat next to him. Jacob's face looked like that of a shunned man. "Jacob, doing a little work to repay a debt can't be as bad as all that."

Jacob shrugged.

Caleb shook the reins. "Giddyap, Snowball." The horse trotted down the drive, past the vegetable garden and out the gate between the white picket fences surrounding the barnyard. Snowball turned right toward Kalona without any coaxing.

"Please be helpful to Sarah." Caleb flashed his warning face at Jacob.

He nodded. "I will. How long do I have to stay and help her?"

Jacob looked deep in thought, worrying his

bottom lip. Caleb regretted his prior words. He knew the *bu* wanted to make amends.

At times Jacob seemed to have a rebellious nature, but Caleb had to trust his *sohn*. "We'll see how much work she has for you to do. Maybe a couple of hours. You can let me know if you get tired."

"Okay."

"But you understand why you must help her, *jah*?"

Jacob put a hand up to shade the sun from his eyes. "I'm working to pay for the cost of the bears I broke."

"Not just that, but the pain and suffering you have caused her. They were the last gift her *ehemann* had given her before he died. Now they're broken. Your helping is just a respectful way of saying you're sorry."

"I'm really sorry I did that."

"I know you are."

They rode in silence but Caleb sensed something different about Jacob. His voice wasn't as cold and distant as it was when they had driven to Kalona last week. He had an obligation now to a very nice woman, and it appeared he accepted the responsibility.

Glancing at the chaos in the bakery's kitchen— containers covering the table, sugar spilled on the counter and pans strewn about—Sarah felt daunted by the mess before her. She brushed the flour from her hands as she checked the time… Running late. Why had she given Hannah the day off? The special order, along with her regular baking, swamped her with work.

Sarah made the last loaf of bread and set it to rise. She grabbed a wet cloth and tidied up her work area. After pushing the utensils to the side, she scooted to the pantry and lugged enough ingredients to the table for six dozen sugar cookies.

Jacob would arrive soon, and she didn't have time to talk or show him what to do. She barely had enough time to get ready to open.

What had she gotten herself into by accepting Caleb's offer for the small *bu* to help…and on a Saturday? Sarah hurried to the front and unlocked the door for Jacob but left the sign on the window turned to Closed.

She'd dirtied almost every pan in the bakery, so maybe Jacob could wash dishes. When he finished with that, they'd figure it out. She'd been meaning to hire extra help but hadn't had time to advertise or interview.

She glanced at the dirty pans in the sink. It would save time if she had clean cookie sheets. She could fetch the spares she'd stored on the top shelf of the built-in cupboard. They were reserved for large orders, like a wedding, but an emergency should warrant the hassle it took to get them down.

Sarah opened the cupboard doors, pulled the step stool over and climbed up. She wasn't quite tall enough for her fingers to touch the shelf next to the ceiling. She stretched. Almost there…but not quite.

Sarah braced a hand on the cupboard and rose to her tiptoes. The pans remained a couple of inches from her grasp. If she stood on the stool's back support, it would give her the boost she needed. She stepped onto the vinyl-covered back and reached for the pans. The stool rocked this way and that way. She flung her arms out, trying to grab hold of the shelf, but missed. She reached for the cupboard door to steady her footing. The stool wiggled, toppled to the right and tossed her straight into a pair of waiting arms and a hard chest.

Arms flailing, she screamed and clutched at his shirt. Her heart galloped against her ribs while she tried to calm down. She gulped a breath.

He dipped his head and his beard tickled her face. Sarah peered up into sage-green eyes and a beaming smile that reached all the way to the corners of his eyes. For once, her brain and tongue failed her simultaneously.

"You could have gotten hurt." Caleb raised his brow, as if waiting for her reply.

A heavy sigh escaped her lips. "*Danki*. You can put me down now." His nearness had created a wild thumping in her chest. When her feet touched the floor, she drew a deep breath and glanced up into his face.

His eyes locked with hers. "Can I trust you to stay on your feet this time?"

She nodded and pulled away from his gaze, trying to calm her runaway heart and snag back her fraying nerves. "Of course. *Danki* for your concern and your help."

Stepping back to regain her composure, she straightened her dress. Then she placed her hands on her prayer *kapp* to make sure it was still secure. She moved it slightly and felt confident of its placement.

Sarah relaxed her shoulders. "Hannah asked for the day off, which has left me to do all the baking, including an extra order for an *Englisch* woman." She turned to Jacob. "What I'd really appreciate right now, if you don't mind, is for you to wash some cookie sheets."

"We'll hang our hats and Jacob will get started." Caleb motioned to Jacob and pointed to the rack by the back door.

Jacob stared at the heap of pans in the sink. Then plunked his hat on a hook, rolled up his sleeves and went to work. Sarah grabbed a towel from the drawer, wrapped it around Jacob's waist and tied it. "This will help protect your clothing."

Caleb raised an eyebrow in a questioning look. "I have some errands to run later. I'll wait out front for a little while to see if you have anything you need me to do, like reaching for something."

"*Danki* for the thought, but I won't be getting on the stool again."

"I didn't mean just that. I could carry a heavy flour sack and refill the bin." The look on his face appeared to be dead serious, except his twitching lips betrayed a suppressed grin.

She flashed him a wry smile. "*Danki*, but we're good for now."

Sarah stole a peek at his back as Caleb returned to the front of the bakery. She touched her hand to her heart and blew out a long breath. How was she ever going to get through the day with him only a few feet away? She clutched the rolling pin to steady her hands.

After she finished the baking, she loaded the cart with cooled pastries, pushed it to the front and transferred them to the display case. Her cheeks warmed as she sensed Caleb's eyes following her every move. "Would you like a cup of coffee and a roll?"

While he ate and read the Amish newspaper, *The Budget*, she continued her morning preparations. When the first customers arrived, Caleb threw his cup away and left to run his errands.

Sarah peered through the doorway at Jacob washing pans and a lump wedged in her throat. It was nice of him to help, even if it was his *daed*'s idea. The pan he was scrubbing looked shiny and clean. He was a hard worker and eager to please. "Customers have come in, so I'll be out front most of the time."

Jacob nodded. "Okay."

While she waited on customers, Jacob pushed the cart out front with sheets of cooled cookies and rolls to replenish the display case. He wiped off the tables, greeted the customers and took dirty dishes to the kitchen without her asking.

When the noontime crowd had disappeared, Sarah was famished. "Now is our slow period, Jacob. How about a peanut butter sandwich and cookie?"

"Okay."

Sarah laid the sandwiches and cookies on plates while Jacob poured himself a glass of milk. They sat at a table by the window and ate in silence as they watched people walk by. She'd often wondered what it would have been like to have a *kind*. At night she sometimes dreamed about one, then woke drenched in tears. Jacob seemed like the perfect little *bu*. He was helpful, sweet and friendly to her customers. It had only been one day but he had already burrowed into her heart, and she didn't want to let him go. Ever.

She swallowed hard. That was a selfish thing to think. *Forgive me, Lord.*

"*Danki*, Jacob, for spending the day. You are a *gut* worker, and I really appreciate your help. In fact, I was so busy that I couldn't have done it without you."

"I'll come back next Saturday."

"You don't have to do that. I'm sure one day's worth of work is enough to pay for the walnut bears."

The doorbell jingled.

"But I *want* to help you." He glanced up at her, his eyes stealing her heart.

She scooted her chair back so she could go wait on the customer. "I can't ask your *daed* to bring you to town again. That would be an imposition. He must be busy and probably needs you at home."

"Please let me help?"

Caleb stepped closer to the table. "You want to what?"

Sarah jerked her head around, surprised to hear Caleb's voice.

"I want to work at the bakery another day to pay my obligation."

"Okay, I'll bring you to Kalona next Saturday."

"Caleb, I hate to ask you to do that. Jacob was

here all morning and worked hard. It's unfair to ask him to come another day."

He looked at Jacob and then at Sarah. "This is the most enthusiastic I've seen him in a year. I have some business in town, so it's no imposition."

She mulled over his offer for a minute. "*Danki*, Caleb."

Jacob flashed her a smile, grabbed his hat and followed his *daed* out the door.

Her heart thrived on the small *bu* and already ached for him. Saturday, she'd get to see them both again.

Caleb turned Snowball into the driveway and headed toward the barn. He couldn't understand the change in the *bu*. Jacob had whistled almost the whole way home.

"Daed, I liked working at the bakery. Sarah said I did a *gut* job." When the buggy stopped, Jacob hopped out. "I'll start chores."

He stared after his *sohn*. What had gotten into him? Perhaps he had eaten too many cookies today and the sugar was giving him a burst of energy.

While he led Snowball to a stall, an image of Sarah fought its way back into his mind. He tried to forget about her smile, about how her small frame had felt in his arms, about how her hair had smelled of peach blossoms. But he couldn't do it.

He couldn't stop thinking about her.

She was a widow. Did she mention that so he'd know? *Nein.* He was sure that was not possible. She only mentioned it because her *ehemann* had made her the bears. Yet a small part of him wanted to think that she wanted him to know.

All week long, Jacob stayed in a *gut* mood. He did all his chores on time and without one complaint. He cleaned his room without Caleb having to ask. In fact, he never saw the *bu* sitting once, only at mealtime and in the evenings. Amazing!

At 5:00 a.m. on Saturday morning, Caleb knocked on Jacob's bedroom door to wake him for chores, and he was surprised to find him dressed and ready to help with the milking. Usually he had to pry the *bu* out of bed. Evidently Jacob was smitten with something at the bakery. Caleb ran a hand through his hair. But what?

The work? Hard to believe.

Sarah? He wouldn't be interested in girls at his age. Yet he did believe Jacob still missed his *mamm.* Sarah had praised the *bu* for doing a *gut* job, as Martha often had. Maybe he needed to do that more, as well.

Jacob helped hitch Snowball to the buggy, then was the first one to hop in the buggy. The closer

Snowball got to town, the faster he trotted and the faster he got his treat of oats.

Caleb's heart rate also increased the closer they got to Kalona. He rubbed his sweaty palms across his thighs. It was too soon for him to think about a *frau*.

Sarah couldn't resist a smile when the bakery door opened. "*Gut* mornin', Jacob. Ready to work again?"

He nodded. "Daed had errands to do and will stop back later."

"*Gut.*" Sarah swiped her hands together to dust the flour off and gave him a pat on the shoulder. "This is Hannah Ropp. She works with me in the bakery."

"Nice to meet you, Jacob." Hannah smiled. "So, you're going to spend your Saturday with us? *Datt* is *wunderbaar*. We can certainly use the help around here."

"Nice to meet you, Hannah." He hung his hat, rolled up his sleeves and dug in to the dirty pans stacked in the sink.

"A man of few words—I like *datt*," Hannah teased.

Sarah finished making the apple pie, sprinkled the top with cinnamon and sugar and then set it in the oven beside the other three pies. She glanced at Jacob, who was busy scrubbing the jelly roll pan. "Jacob, what would you like to do when you grow up? Farm like your *daed*?"

"Be a baker like you."

Sarah paused. She hadn't expected that. *"Jah?"* She turned toward Jacob. "You could come and work with Hannah and me. We'd like that, wouldn't we, Hannah?"

"Of course we would." She laughed.

"My *daed* was a baker, Jacob. This was his bakery. I worked here every day after school, helping him." Sarah finished kneading the dough, set the mound of wheat bread into a pan, covered it and set it off to the side to rise.

"After Mamm died, the bakery was the place Daed, my brother Turner and I worked together as a family. After Daed and my husband, Samuel, died, the bakery, Hannah and our customers became my family. Turner took over Daed's woodworking shop. Now he's too busy to stop by much."

"I didn't think I'd seen Turner in here lately." Hannah tossed her a curious look.

"Jah. He usually stopped in for a roll and coffee a couple of times a week, but not lately. Maybe he had extra woodworking orders with summer and the *Englischers'* wedding season close."

Jacob finished washing pans, swept the floors and then trotted to the front and wiped off tables.

He laughed with Sarah and Hannah when a lull in customers permitted it.

Sarah snatched little glances of Jacob as he worked. He was a *wunderbaar* little *bu*, and she enjoyed his company. "Jacob, did your *mamm* bake you cookies?"

"*Jah*, Mamm was a *gut* baker. She made all kinds of cookies and pies. On my birthday, she'd make me a cake. She made a quilt for my bed. It had squares on it and each one had a different-shaped leaf made out of autumn-colored fabric. When I was sick one time, she sat up all night beside my bed." His voice cracked and he wiped a tear from his cheek.

Sarah's heart wept as she sensed Jacob missed his *mamm* and craved the attention of a mother figure. She had experienced that before when other *kinner* in her church had lost a parent. Perhaps she could fill the void for Jacob in some way.

Maybe his *daed* didn't see Jacob's need to confide in a woman. On the other hand, maybe he did and that was the reason why he agreed to bring Jacob to work with her in the bakery.

Late morning, Caleb pushed open the bakery door, and Sarah met him at the counter. "Would you like a cookie and a cup of coffee before you head home?"

"*Datt* would be nice. Would you sit with me at a table for a few minutes?"

"*Jah*. I have a little time. Especially now since I have two good workers in the bakery." She said it in a voice a bit louder than normal and glanced over her shoulder at Jacob to see if he had heard.

She caught the little smile pulling at the corners of Jacob's mouth as he tried to hold it back.

Her heart stuttered at Caleb's nearness. She handed him a cookie on a plate, poured two cups of coffee and then followed him to a table. When she sat, her gaze met his. His sage-green eyes held hers as tightly as his two strong arms had last Saturday. A rush of warmth flooded her cheeks as she remembered that moment.

"I hope Jacob helped some. He's a small *bu* and has his limitations."

"Jacob is a fabulous worker. He washed pans, mopped the floor, cleaned tables, loaded trays on the cart and pushed it out front. He's a great help and strong, too. Does he do a lot of work at home?"

"His sister, Mary, who's thirteen, does the housework. Jacob works outside, mostly in the garden. When he gets older, he'll farm with me."

"I see. Is that what he wants to do?"

"What boy doesn't want to work alongside his *daed*?" Caleb's smile reflected a fatherly elation.

"*Jah*, indeed, but sometimes *kinner* want to go their own way and try something new."

Brushing off the temptation to enlighten him

that Jacob preferred the bakery to farming, she sipped her coffee and held her tongue. It wasn't her place to do so, and besides Jacob could change his mind. It might just be a novelty for him to work in a bakery. Something different than cleaning a dirty barn.

Jacob and Hannah both let out a laugh.

"I haven't heard him laugh since his *mamm* died. It's doing him *gut* to come and work here."

"Hannah and I enjoyed having him." She turned and faced the kitchen. "Jacob, your *daed* is here for you."

Jacob strolled to the front of the bakery and stopped at the end of the table.

"I heard you worked hard for Sarah. Are you ready to go home?" Caleb stood and picked up his hat.

Jacob's eyes sparkled. "*Nein*. I'd like to stay and live with Sarah at the bakery and work for her. She asked me to."

Shocked, Sarah looked at Caleb's face. His eyes widened and his mouth gaped. She turned her gaze back to Jacob. Had she heard him correctly?

She stood and faced Caleb to explain. But his complexion had turned ashen and his hat slipped from his hands and dropped to the floor.

Chapter Four

Still reeling from Jacob's announcement that he wanted to live with her, Sarah pressed a hand to her chest. Without saying a word, Caleb retrieved his hat from the floor. He straightened and glanced at her, his eyes dewy like the forest during a heavy mist.

The bell jingled as the bakery door pushed open and an elderly couple entered. Hannah rushed to greet the customers, nodding to Sarah and indicating she had this. Sarah blew out a breath. She didn't want to delay this conversation.

Caleb's skin above his whiskered cheeks had turned cherry-red. His six-foot stature seemed shorter as his shoulders slumped with the weight of his *sohn*'s brutal words. The man's eyes reflected his world crumbling like a day-old cookie.

Sarah drew a sharp breath and prepared to deal with what she had started. "Let's sit a minute."

Since the tables were empty, she motioned toward the corner table so customers wouldn't overhear their conversation. It also gave her a second longer to decide how to explain this misunderstanding to Caleb. He probably believed she had meddled in his life.

The late-afternoon sun and heat streamed through the window, intensifying her discomfort. She blotted the moisture clinging to her neck with her hand as the guys slid behind the table.

Sarah leaned behind Jacob and pulled the cord on the blind, her mind racing about how to approach the subject. She scooted out the chair directly opposite from Caleb and sat.

How was she going to explain that his *sohn* would rather work in the bakery than on the farm? Not something an Amish man wanted to hear, or probably any man, if he had his heart set on it. She swiped her palms on her apron as she directed her attention across the table.

Caleb glanced down and raised his forearms to the table with his calloused, weathered-roughened hands outstretched in front of him. He sucked in a loud breath and cut his eyes to his *bu*.

Jacob sat next to Caleb, acting as if he were unaware of the impact his words had had on his *daed*. The *bu*'s small body scooted up next to the table, with only the tops of his shoulders and head visible above the table.

"Sweetie." Sarah looked at Jacob and whispered. "When we talked about you working in the bakery, I meant when you had grown and finished school."

"But you said you worked in your *daed*'s bakery every day after school and liked it because you were in a family. I want to be part of a family, too." His tiny voice started to tremble.

"I'm sorry that you misunderstood."

Sarah raised her eyes to Caleb, imploring his help. She realized Jacob was desperately seeking what he'd lost, and her heart was breaking for him.

Caleb remained silent. By the pitiful look on his face, it was as if his *sohn* had asked for a divorce from his family.

Jacob's words sliced through Caleb's heart like a steel blade, then plunged to the very depth of his soul.

A shiver coursed through his body. After Martha's death, he'd stayed late in the fields and lingered cleaning tools so exhaustion would consume him at bedtime. That helped Caleb deal with the grief. But without giving it a thought, he'd let his *kinner* struggle with their *mamm*'s death on their own. What had he been thinking? Then he'd scolded Jacob when he relaxed by the pond. Instead, he should have taken a few minutes to lie with the *bu* in the grass.

He reached over, enfolded Jacob's hand into his and squeezed gently. "Jacob, we can't ask Sarah to let you live with her. She is busy with her bakery and probably doesn't have an extra bedroom in her apartment."

"But Daed, I could help her and sleep in her bakery."

"*Nein*, that won't work, Jacob. You can't sleep in the bakery. When she needs help, I will drive you into town to help her. I know Sarah is your friend and you would like to spend more time with her. What would you say if we invited her out to our farm for dinner next Sunday?"

His face glowed. "*Jah*, okay."

"Sarah. If you are available for dinner, Jacob and I would be honored to drive into Kalona and escort you to our home."

"*Jah*, I would like *datt*." She turned toward Jacob. "When I come to your house, I'll scrub *your* sink full of pans."

Jacob laughed. "Okay, but I'll help you."

"*Datt* sounds *gut*. Go tell Hannah I said for her to bag some cookies for you to take home." Jacob ran to the back of the bakery.

"Caleb, I'm so sorry. Jacob and I were having a casual conversation as we worked. I told him about working with my family in the bakery after school. I didn't realize he took it a different way. What I didn't tell Jacob was my *daed* was very strict and my *bruder* and I worked hard from a very early age. But I liked helping in the bakery and didn't mind."

"I understand. Jacob's *mamm* died a year ago, and he still misses her. Martha's death had a devastating impact on the *bu*, and I failed to notice it. I stay in the fields too late and don't spend enough time with the *kinner*. That'll change." He stood, retrieved his hat from the peg and nodded to Sarah as he headed for the door.

Jacob dragged his feet as he made his way to the front of the bakery, a smile touching the corners of the *bu*'s mouth as he said goodbye to Sarah, but it disappeared and was replaced by a sadness that Caleb worried wouldn't go away.

Caleb followed Jacob into the house, hurrying to catch up. For a six-year-old, he could surely outrun his *daed*.

Jacob held the sack up. "Mary, I have some cookies from the bakery. We can share."

Mary shrugged at her brother, rolled her eyes, then finished making a pie and placed it in the oven.

"Guess what, Mary? Sarah is coming to dinner next Sunday, and we get to cook for her!"

Mary stopped and glared at Jacob. "Is that so? Am I the one who will be cooking dinner?"

Caleb cleared his throat. "We will all make dinner together for our guest. It doesn't have to be anything fancy."

"You mean *your* guest." She shoved the laundry basket of clothes she'd been folding to the corner. Then grabbed the pot holders and pulled the cornbread out of the oven.

The assault of ammonia and floor cleaner tipped Caleb off to how hard Mary had been working since they took off for town. The house was clean, the table set for dinner, and the steamy whiff of ham and candied sweet potatoes smelled *gut*.

He hadn't noticed before, but Mary's feelings were sensitive, too. She'd had a deep attachment to her *mamm*, and bringing another woman into her home was going to meet with resistance, no doubt.

Mary was a thirteen-year-old going on thirty. She never complained; she just did what had to be done. Caleb moved out of her way as she dished up dinner in silence. He hung his hat on a peg by the door and dragged his hand through his hair to smooth it down. Apparently neither Jacob nor Mary was happy. Their lives had fallen apart since Martha's death, and it was all his fault.

He had to give his *kinner* a loving home. Martha would have been disappointed in his behavior. He treated Mary and Jacob like adults. He needed to let them be *kinner*. Maybe he could hire someone occasionally to help with the household chores.

The next morning Caleb tried to help Mary whenever he could. He made Jacob pick up more responsibility around the house, as well. The week passed with little complaining or talking of any kind from Mary. She said what was necessary and not a word more.

On Saturday Caleb watched as Jacob helped make sugar cookies. He dusted the table with flour, as Mary did. Rolled out his dough and used a round cookie cutter to stamp out shapes. Caleb walked over to survey the work, his shoes crunching over the sugarcoated wood flooring.

"When I grow up, Mary, I'm going to work with Sarah in her bakery." Jacob slid a spatula under the dough and set each cookie on a baking sheet.

Mary glanced at Jacob and rolled her eyes.

Caleb prayed Sunday dinner would go off without any problems.

On Sunday Caleb peeled and cut potatoes and carrots while Mary prepared the roast. When everything was almost ready, he and Jacob hitched

Snowball and rode to Kalona to fetch Sarah. The whole way there, Jacob made plans for Sarah's visit.

Yet a slight uneasiness bubbled in Caleb's belly. Mary had offered no conversation while they worked in the kitchen this morning. Was she still brooding about cooking for their guest?

When they pulled up, Sarah was ready in front of the bakery. Caleb walked her to the buggy. Just as she stepped up to the carriage, she jerked her head at the sound of wheels and horses' hooves pounding the paved road as a buggy approached.

"*Ach.* Melinda Miller." She gave her a wave, then accepted Caleb's help to step up. "She'll be sure to tell everyone she saw me getting into your buggy."

Caleb waved his hand in a dismissive manner. "It's Visiting Sunday, and you're going visiting."

"*Jah*, that's true," she reasoned.

When he pulled into his driveway, Sarah's gaze bounced from the gardens to the fields. "It's a lovely farm, Caleb."

"*Danki.*" He helped her out of the buggy and escorted her up the porch steps.

Jacob grabbed her hand. "I'll show you my room."

Sarah turned and gave Caleb a shrug. "Guess I have a tour guide with an itinerary for the day."

"Slow down, Jacob. Show Sarah your room

while I unhitch Snowball. Then we must eat before anything else. Mary will have dinner ready." Caleb's stomach had been rumbling for the past hour, and he didn't want Mary's hard work on dinner to go to waste. He hurried to unhook Snowball, walked the horse to his stall and then hurried back to the *haus*.

Caleb hung his hat on the hook, washed his hands and, while Mary poured the cold milk, he carried the food to the table. "Jacob and Sarah. Time to eat."

Jacob led his guest to the table and pulled out a chair. "This is where you sit."

"Danki." Sarah made herself comfortable.

Caleb motioned to Mary. "This is my *tochter*, Mary." Then he turned to Sarah. "This is Sarah Gingerich from the Amish Sweet Delights bakery."

Mary gave Sarah a slight nod.

Sarah reached out to shake Mary's hand, but Mary stepped back. "Sorry, my hand may have grease on it from the roast. I wouldn't want you to get any on your hands or your dress."

"Mary. Please wash your hands." Caleb tossed her a warning look. He knew Mary's stubborn nature. She wouldn't warm up to Sarah until she was ready, but he wouldn't stand for her offensive behavior.

She washed her hands at the sink, came back

and offered a hand to Sarah. "*Hullo*, Sarah. *Welkum*." Mary's words hit their destination like icy pellets.

Caleb exhaled. It was going to be a long afternoon. "Shall we all join hands for prayer?" He said the blessing, then passed the serving platter around the table.

"*Ach*. New Order Amish pray aloud at the table. We do not." Sarah gasped.

"*Jah*. On the off-Sundays when the church doesn't have preaching, the New Order Amish have open Bible study and Sunday school to deepen our personal relationship with *Gott* and our assurance of salvation."

"*Ach*. Old Order still clings to the adage that only the church interprets scripture, and beyond living a godly life and working hard, we can only have hope of our salvation." Sarah took a bite of food and turned to Mary. "Mmm, this roast is delicious."

"*Danki*."

"Did your *mamm* teach you how to cook?"

"Of course."

The heat from Mary's rude words burned on Caleb's cheeks. He'd hoped Mary would like Sarah. *Apparently that's not going to happen.* "Sarah, Jacob and I have a little surprise for you after dinner."

"I like surprises. That sounds like fun."

When they were finished eating, Sarah jumped up, began clearing the table and carrying the dishes to the sink. Caleb helped Sarah while Mary put the condiments and leftover food away, then joined Sarah at the sink.

"Sit, Caleb, finish your coffee. You too, Mary. You cooked. I'll wash the dishes." Sarah motioned them toward the table.

"*Danki*, but you came to visit with Daed and Jacob. Go visit with them. I'll take care of the dishes."

"*Nein*. We'll all pitch in to get them done faster. Jacob and I'll help, too." Caleb grabbed a dish towel. "I can't believe you were going to pass up the help, Mary."

Defiance glowed in Mary's eyes as they darted at Caleb. But she remained silent.

Sarah took a step back after the last dish found its way to the cupboard. She understood Mary wasn't going to let her, or probably any woman, into her kitchen. If Caleb made Mary step aside for a *frau*, she'd do it, but begrudgingly.

After Jacob finished sweeping the floor clean of crumbs and set the broom away, he ran to Caleb. "Now, Daed?"

"*Jah*. Now we take Sarah on the tour." Caleb opened the door and swept his arm toward the outside. "Your tour is about to begin, Frau Gingerich."

They walked her around the flower and vegetable gardens, then stopped by the barn for her to meet Tiger, the cat. When he rubbed against her leg, she picked him up. "You're a real beauty."

He purred in response.

Jacob tugged at her arm as excitement set his feet to prancing. "Come on, we have a surprise." Jacob walked her to the pen where the newborn calf laid next to his *mamm*.

"Oh, he is gorgeous." Sarah gave Caleb a glance when he stood next to her.

The cat jumped out of Sarah's arms, squeezed through the board fence and rubbed up against the calf.

"Ah, even Tiger likes him." The innocence of the animals warmed her heart.

"There's one last place to see. I'll give you a hint." Jacob rubbed his chin with his hand like he was deep in thought. "It's a great spot on a hot day."

Sarah looked up toward the sky as if really pondering the question, then dropped her gaze back to Jacob. "I have no idea what it is. Lead the way."

Jacob traipsed through the grass and weeds along the bank to the grove of maple trees by the pond on the edge of the pasture. Jacob pointed to the water, his face beaming.

"Oh! What a wonderful place to relax on the

grass." She looked around. "It's a beautiful farm, Caleb and Jacob, and so well kept."

Both their faces glowed with pride.

"I contract the fields of vegetables to canneries, and I grow extra to sell at the auction and market." He turned around and pointed to the north pasture. "And we have a few milk cows."

"*Jah*, I see but it looks like more than a few."

"About forty."

"The farm must keep you busy."

Caleb nodded. "*Jah*, it does."

She couldn't keep her eyes off him. He was a handsome man, with a charming way about him. Even with a beard, she could see his strong jaw. She liked his beard. The New Order men kept theirs trimmed, while the Old Order didn't allow such things. Her stomach fluttered whenever Caleb spoke to her, as though she were a young girl who was in a courtship with a *bu*. Only, now it was a man with *kinner*.

"Daed, is it time for cookies?" Jacob turned toward Sarah. "I helped make them."

"Then I definitely want one." Sarah wrapped her arm around Jacob's shoulder. "Lead the way, Mr. Baker."

The aroma of freshly brewed coffee greeted them when they entered the kitchen. Mary had the cookies and plates on the table. "Mmm, smells *gut* in here. You are a *wunderbaar* hostess, Mary."

"Danki." Mary nodded as she pulled out a chair from the table and sat.

Dessert was light and quick. And Sarah was thankful. She finished her coffee and cookie, then brushed the crumbs from her skirt.

Caleb excused himself to go hitch the horse to the buggy. "I'll meet you out front in a few minutes, Sarah."

"Jah, danki. I'll be ready."

Sarah stood. "Goodbye, Mary. I enjoyed meeting you."

Mary didn't stand. "Nice to meet you, too, Sarah." Her tone didn't match her congenial words.

A cold shimmy worked its way up Sarah's back. Could it be more obvious? She wasn't welcome in Mary's house.

Chapter Five

The ringing of the doorbell pulled Sarah's attention away from the display case and stopped her urge to eat a pecan roll. Her brother walked through the front door. "Turner, it's *gut* to see you."

He sauntered toward her. "Likewise, sister."

She dashed around the counter and tugged him into a hug. "Where have you been the past few weeks?"

"The shop keeps me busy." He tilted his chin up and breathed deeply. "Mmm. I forgot how *gut* it smells in here. I'll take one of Papa's cinnamon-nut rolls and a cup of coffee."

"Hey, Turner." Hannah poked her head out of the kitchen doorway. "Quit being a stranger. We miss you."

"*Jah*, I'm watching my waistline. Trying to get healthier. Can't keep eating rolls every day for breakfast."

"Okay, but don't talk like that in here, or you'll ruin our business. It's a *gut* thing you're our first customer." Hannah laughed as she disappeared back into the kitchen.

Sarah smiled as she listened to their banter. Her unmarried friend had hidden her crush on Turner for years. If he knew, he'd never acted on it these five years since he'd been a widower. She had wanted to let it slip to him, but Hannah made her promise to keep it a secret.

"Here's your sweet roll. I'll bring your coffee to the table." A few minutes later, Sarah set the cup down in front of him.

"Can you sit a minute and talk?" Turner's face looked serious, like the time he told her that their *daed* had died.

She pulled out a chair and sat opposite him. "*Jah*, I can stay until customers start coming. Hannah is baking, so I have to cover the counter. We miss you. Stop more often, even if you don't get a roll and coffee."

"*Jah*. I'll try. Sarah, there has been talk around the community about you."

She stared at her brother. "What talk? You mean about the bakery or me?"

He lowered his voice. "Both. They're saying a New Order Amish man and his *bu* have been hanging around the bakery. Word is that you went to his farm. Is that true?"

Her stomach clenched. Melinda Miller saw her getting into Caleb's buggy, and evidently someone saw her at his farm. "*Jah*, but it's not what you're implying."

"You should never go to a man's farm by yourself. What were you thinking?"

"Jacob, Caleb's *sohn* broke Samuel's bears, and Caleb wanted Jacob to work in the bakery to make amends. His *mamm* died, and he was looking for..." She shifted in her chair.

"For what? A *mamm*? It looks bad for a woman to go to a man's farm unescorted. You know that. He's New Order. You don't want to marry outside our church. You complain now about not seeing me. Our church would shun you. New Order approves the use of tractors, lawn mowers, inside flush toilets, mechanical milkers, refrigerators and telephones in their homes that are not in accordance with our *Ordnung*. They're too progressive. If I ever have a *kind*, I wouldn't want him hanging around New Order *kinner* of families that have these conveniences. They spoil their youngies with those contraptions and get them used to the outside world. Yet it's the Old Order that boasts around a twenty percent higher youth retention rate."

Heat worked its way up her neck and burned on her cheeks. Sarah clenched her fists. "We're only friends. You are blowing this out of proportion. I'm not leaving our church."

"Watch yourself, sister. Your actions reflect on me, too." His eyes turned cold and locked with hers.

She held his gaze. "I run a business. They're customers."

"Be careful, Sarah. You could get disciplined by the bishop. Then the Amish will avoid your bakery."

She held her shaking hands up, palms out. "Stop it."

"Nein. *I'm* warning *you*. There's been talk." His tone sliced the air like a sharpened knife.

Silence stretched out between them, then he moved his gaze from her to the plate sitting before him.

He took a bite of roll. "Not bad. Daed's were better."

Jah, of course. To her *bruder*, she'd never bake or run the bakery as well as Daed had. Sarah straightened her back. The door opened and she rose. She gave Turner a quick smile.

"*Danki* for stopping." She called back over her shoulder. Her stomach turned queasy. He was telling her to do something she didn't want to do. Now she knew how Mary Brenneman felt when Caleb wanted her to like the woman he brought home.

Betrayed.

* * *

The morning was exhausting. A long break at lunch improved her mood, but Sarah kept rehashing Turner's words in her head. How could she convince her brother and the bishop that she and Caleb were just friends?

She emptied the carafe, yanked the coffee-grounds' basket out of its holder and spilled the wet grounds on the floor. What a mess!

She wiped up the grounds, mopped the floor and brewed a fresh pot. When the doorbell jingled, a group of five women entered. They were tourists. It was obvious from the tour-guide pamphlets in their hands. Sarah held out a plate of sample cookies. "*Welkum*, would you like to try a cookie?" When a woman reached out to take one, she bumped the plate, sending it crashing to the floor and breaking to smithereens.

"Oh, I'm so sorry. I'll be glad to pay for the plate."

"That's not necessary. I break a lot of plates, too." Sarah hurried and swept up the pieces.

The woman purchased two loaves of bread, a cherry pie and two dozen of Sarah's new lemon cookies, which she raved about after trying the sample.

Ach, she must have felt guilty. She bought enough to pay for a dozen plates. "*Danki* for stopping by."

Ten minutes to closing, Sarah walked the last

customer to the door and peeked out the window. Dark clouds bumped and gathered, slowly squeezing the light from the day. Thunder rumbled like the moan of creation and lightning sliced across the ominous sky.

Streams of rain covered the window while the brooding sky churned and howled. Horses' hooves sloshing through water pulled her gaze to the street in time to see a buggy skid to a stop in front of her shop. *Nein.* A stifled groan stuck in her throat.

Bishop Yoder jumped out, dashed to the bakery and pushed the door open.

"*Gut* afternoon, Sarah." He removed his hat, pulled a handkerchief from his pocket and wiped the water from his face.

"*Jah*, the same to you. You couldn't make it home before the storm broke loose?"

"*Nein*, but I wanted to stop by and talk to you anyway. It's almost closing, *jah*?"

"I was getting ready to flip the sign over."

He turned to the door and flipped the card dangling from a string. "Done."

"*Danki.*" The pit of her stomach dropped.

"Let's have a seat and talk." He swept his hand toward a table.

Heat burned her cheeks as she pulled a chair out and sat. Averting her eyes from his face, she studied her clasped hands in her lap. Was Turner right? Was he here to discipline her? Wait. How did Turner know? As the oldest male of their family and the owner of the bakery, had the bishop talked to him first?

She sensed the bishop's stare. *Nein*, she hadn't done anything wrong. After all, she had a business and needed to be civil to her customers. Even accepting an occasional dinner invitation to help heal a brokenhearted *kind* should be her right. She raised her eyes to meet the bishop's stare.

"Sarah, it has reached my ears that you visited a New Order man's farm, unescorted."

"Bishop, have you heard the old saying? 'Believe none of what you hear and only half of what you see.'"

"Do not fraternize with him, or you could find yourself disciplined. Some of their beliefs and practices are not in accordance with our *Ordnung*." His tone turned haughty. "Be careful, Sarah. Some think you need to confess."

"I'm not courting Caleb Brenneman. We are only friends. His *sohn* broke the bears that sat on the bakery's counter and he worked in the bakery for his discipline. The *bu* is still mourning the death of his *mamm* and having a difficult time adjusting. Little Jacob took a shine to me, and they asked me to dinner to say *danki*. That's all. I've done nothing shameful."

"As a young widow, you need a family of your

own. Alvin Studer needs a wife and a *mamm* for his six *kinner*. It would be a good match for both of you." Bishop Yoder set his elbows on the table and clasped his hands as if he were praying. "It's not *gut* for a young woman to be by herself. You need an *ehemann, jah*?"

She knew the direction he was heading. There would be no discipline if she married Alvin. It was unsaid, but it was there between the words.

"Alvin is only a few years older than you."

"Twelve years." She glared at the bishop.

"And he would make you a *gut* spouse. Unlike Caleb Brenneman, Alvin is Old Order."

The rain burst from the sky in a torrential downpour. Sarah glanced out the window. *Lord, please stop the rain so the bishop can go home.* "I don't *liebe* Alvin."

"After you're married, *liebe* will come, I'm sure." The bishop's mouth was set in a firm line.

A sliver of golden glow squeezed through the window blind. Sarah witnessed the sun peeking through the clouds. The rain had suddenly stopped. *Danki, Lord.* Sarah scooted her chair back and stood.

"*Danki* for stopping by, Bishop Yoder, but I've stood on my feet all day and I'm tired. You have given me much to think about." She strolled to the door and opened it for her guest.

He nodded to Sarah on his way out the door.

"Alvin needs to get married soon." His deep, solemn tone grated on her ear.

His piercing gaze tried to rip through her resolve and jab at her heart. Did he think she was going to give up the bakery to marry a man whom she didn't *liebe* and take care of his six *kinner*?

Sarah shoved the door closed, maybe a little too hard. The bishop glanced back over his shoulder. She locked the dead bolt, then swallowed a lump of frustration. She wadded up the bishop's plan for her life into an imaginary ball and let it roll over her shoulder and down her back.

A pan banging in the kitchen startled Sarah. She turned as Hannah appeared at the kitchen door.

"Is he gone?" Hannah slowly moved into the front of the bakery.

"Jah."

"I'm sorry. I overheard."

"I figured you had."

"What are you going to do?" Hannah wiped her hands across her apron.

"He threatened to discipline me, but I've no intention of marrying Alvin Studer."

"I'm afraid you two are going to butt heads," Hannah said, wearing a grave face.

Sarah nodded. *Lord God, what are You truly asking of me?*

* * *

On Saturday Caleb pushed the Amish Sweet Delights door open and followed Jacob inside. Sarah glanced up from arranging pastries in the display case and tossed them a weak smile. Her eyes darted to the tables, then back at them as they approached the counter. Had he said something to offend her? This wasn't her normal greeting.

Jacob sprinted behind the counter and gave Sarah a hug. "I've missed you."

She leaned down, patted his back and whispered, "Me, too, sweetie." He ran back around the counter to start his hunt for the perfect treat.

Caleb's heart began to thump as he approached Sarah. "*Gut* mornin'. I'll take a frosted cinnamon roll and a cup of coffee."

She nodded and smiled at him, but she had an air of coolness about her. The week was a long, busy one for him but daydreaming of seeing her today had gotten him through. Now she seemed disinterested or tired. His throat tightened. "Have you had a busy morning, Sarah?"

She pulled a roll out of the display case, placed it on a plate and pushed it across the counter toward him. She poured his coffee, handed it to him, leaned in and whispered, "At the corner table are the bishop and some Elders from my church. They're watching me and wanted to know about our relationship. They don't like that we're friends."

"We will go," he mouthed silently.

Jacob chimed in. "I'll have the cream-filled donut and milk, please."

"Good choice." Sarah smiled at the *bu*. "They are especially *gut* today. Why don't you get that empty table, and I'll bring it over." Jacob ran to the table and sat.

As she arranged their order on a tray, she whispered to Caleb, "*Nein*. Jacob might say something if you just leave. I'll refill coffee cups and talk a minute. Maybe you could leave after that."

He carried their treats to the table, sat and gave Jacob his plate. To the *Englisch*, the Plain communities were the same. But that wasn't true. The Old Order had a problem with many of the conveniences that his New Order used, and his church believed in evangelizing. The Old Order communities didn't agree with that kind of mingling. Caleb hadn't thought living in such close proximity to the Old Order would make that much of a difference. And it wouldn't have if it weren't for his continued relationship with Sarah.

Yet he enjoyed her company. They were friends. *That's all.* Jacob adored her. Sarah had mended the *bu*'s heart, and he didn't want to pull that stitching out.

Sarah waited a few minutes before walking

around with the coffee carafe. She stopped at the bishop's table and refilled their cups. "I don't often get Elders in here. I hope you enjoyed your coffee and rolls and will come back. Abraham, I remember you teasing me as a child when you stopped by to see Daed. It's *gut* to see you in the bakery again." Sarah's voice carried and Caleb could overhear the conversation.

"*Jah*, I remember those days. I miss coming here and visiting with your *daed*," Abraham said fondly.

"I miss those days, too," Sarah agreed.

She moved to the next table and gave a friendly smile. "Are you visiting Kalona?"

The woman nodded.

"Yep, we have our tour guide right here." The man held up the newest Kalona tourist pamphlet.

"I've seen that. It is a *gut* guide. There's a lot to see. Be sure to stop by the artisan shop. It has many *wunderbaar* things. Have a *gut* day." Sarah flashed them her best smile.

She stopped at Caleb's table. "I'm glad to see you, Jacob. Is your garden growing tall with all the rain this past week?"

"*Jah*. Everything has come up, and we will soon have vegetables to eat. You should come out and see it."

Caleb could see her face redden.

"*Jah*, maybe Hannah and I can visit soon. I enjoyed seeing you both, but I need to get back to the counter. Have a *gut* day."

She turned to leave, but Jacob started to ask Sarah something. "*Nein,* Jacob. We need to be on our way. Have a *gut* day, Sarah."

A loud bang came from the kitchen. Sarah set the pot on the counter and ran to the back. Caleb and Jacob jumped up and followed her to the kitchen.

Hannah looked up, startled. "I'm sorry. The rack holding the pans came loose from the wall when I pulled a pan off. I hope I didn't scare everyone." Her voice quaked. Hannah bent and started to pick up the mess.

Caleb and Jacob hurried to help clear the floor.

"Don't worry about it. I'm glad you're not hurt." Sarah took some pans from Hannah and set them on the counter.

Hannah stood and placed her hands on her waist. "I meant to tell Turner when he came in the next time that the rack was loose."

"You could have gotten hurt." Caleb picked up a couple of pans and set them by the sink. "Let me know when something needs repair. It won't take long. I can do it when I'm in town."

Caleb looked at Sarah. "I'll fix the rack right now. Do you have a screwdriver and screws?"

She pulled a toolbox from the closet. "This should have what you need."

He pulled the step stool over and got busy. Sarah watched the counter out front but stuck her head back in the kitchen to see how the work progressed.

While Caleb rehung the rack, Jacob helped Hannah clean the floor of stuff that had spilled when the pans hit the stove and counter. Caleb was proud of the way Jacob had matured since he'd started helping at the bakery. It confirmed he'd made the right decision.

After securing the rack to the wall, Caleb examined all the cupboard doors and shelves. He poked his nose into the pantry and checked the organizer.

He stepped into the front of the bakery. "It's fixed, Sarah."

She glanced back in the kitchen. *"Wunderbaar."*

"I noticed there are a couple of loose cupboard doors and wobbly shelves. I'll come back another day when you're not so busy and fix them."

"That sounds *gut*."

Caleb put the toolbox away, tidied up, and on their way out Sarah handed Jacob a sack of cookies. *"Danki* for all your work."

He and Jacob grabbed their hats and headed for the front door. Caleb faced the corner table and nodded. The bishop nodded back but the Elders stared at him with stony faces.

The pit of his stomach flopped. It appeared they were determined not to lose one of their flock.

As they headed to the buggy, Caleb heard low voices speaking behind him. He glanced over his shoulder and locked eyes with the bishop. Next to him walked the Elders. Were they planning to have a talk with him? Caleb stubbed his shoe on an uneven spot in the sidewalk and almost stumbled.

Snowball was half a block down the street, and when the horse saw them, he shuffled his hooves around, ready to stretch his legs. As Caleb stepped into the buggy, he caught a glimpse of the men on the sidewalk. The bishop nodded as he passed. The Elders looked straight ahead as if they never saw them.

Jah. He got the message. Loud and clear.

Chapter Six

Sarah placed her elbows close to the table's edge, with her hands folded and propped under her chin. She couldn't decide which she dreaded more. The Elders and Caleb seated in the bakery at the same time or leaving at the same time.

Hannah pushed a steaming cup of cinnamon-spice coffee and a sticky maple-pecan roll in front of Sarah, and sat down opposite her. "You look like you've just given away your last kitten. Monday morning blahs?"

"I'm still worrying about the bishop and the Elders following Caleb out of the bakery last Saturday. The bishop wouldn't dare say anything to Caleb. Would he?"

"He might. He doesn't think the Plain community should have modern conveniences or be studying the Bible. To him, the Bible is for the church to interpret."

"What should I say to the bishop?"

"Nothing. Caleb can take care of himself. Eat the roll. It's delicious."

Sarah sniffed the gooey maple and toasted pecans smothering the yeast roll, then took a bite. "Mmm." She smiled and nodded.

"I knew you'd like it."

Sarah chewed and swallowed. "In some ways, I don't fault the bishop." She blotted her mouth with a napkin. "He's trying to keep his community happy and together. It's fine to introduce widows and widowers if they want someone to marry. I know Alvin wants a *frau*, but it's not going to be me." She took another bite of the roll.

"Why don't you ask Turner to talk to the bishop on your behalf?" Hannah suggested as she sipped her coffee.

"It's been three years since my *ehemann* died. I loved Samuel, but he had a take-charge attitude. I've enjoyed my independence and making my own decisions since he's been gone. I've been satisfied working in the bakery. I would have liked *kinner*, but I have *nein* intention of leaving my bakery or my faith."

"At least you were married. I can't even say that. It's a wonder Bishop Yoder isn't asking *me* to marry Alvin instead of you." Hannah dunked her pastry in her coffee. "Of course, if I'd quit eating these..." She chuckled and held up her roll.

"I could probably snag a man, but I do love to eat and don't mind wearing a larger size."

Sarah settled back in her chair. "I don't love Alvin and don't want a man that hits his *frau*. Caleb is New Order, and I can't marry him or I'll be shunned."

"You need an *ehemann* to share your life. And maybe you could have *kinner* with another man. Who knows?" Hannah shrugged.

"If that happened, I would feel like I betrayed Samuel."

"Don't say that. Samuel would want you to be happy." Hannah took the last bite of her roll.

Sarah wiped her hands on a napkin. "Besides, I enjoy the bakery. I don't know what I'd do without it. Caleb's only been a widower for a year. I'm not sure he wants a permanent relationship."

The doorbell rang and Sarah pushed her problem with the bishop to the back of her mind as she walked to the counter. Hannah shot her a smile as she cleared the table and scampered back to the kitchen.

Catching the door as the customer left, Caleb skirted around her and entered. His face drawn, lines covered his forehead, his eyes rimmed in red with dark circles below them.

Sarah rushed around the counter and motioned him toward a table. She set a cinnamon roll and coffee in front of him. "What's wrong, Caleb?" Sarah patted his shoulder and sat beside him.

"My *bruder* got hurt Saturday. I've been at the hospital ever since I heard. He's in the ICU in Iowa City. A drunk driver in an SUV hit his buggy. Peter has internal bleeding, broken bones, head injuries and he's in a coma." Caleb took a deep breath. "The *kinner* and I were there all day yesterday and last night. They were tired and bored, so I brought them home. I have a favor to ask, Sarah. If you can't or don't want to do it, I'll understand. But I was wondering if you could come to the farm today and stay with the *kinner* while I go back to the hospital."

"Sure, we're only open until noon on Mondays. Hannah can close up."

"Glad to do it." Hannah said as she walked toward the table.

Sarah started for the kitchen. "I'll get my bag while you finish eating. Then we can go."

In Caleb's buggy, Sarah tried her best to shrink out of sight from the people walking on the sidewalk. When a buggy approached from the opposite direction, she tipped her head down.

This wasn't right. Why should she have to act like a thief in the dark when she wanted to help a friend? Yet was she prepared if someone from her church saw her and sent the bishop to her door again?

Sarah glanced at Caleb and noticed how close his body was to hers. *Ach.* She needed to take her mind off him. He hadn't said a word since they had climbed into the buggy. Worry lines etched deep in his face signaled he was thinking of his *bruder.* She gazed at the landscape, the sky painted with a veil of thin clouds and a light fog still hovering, concealing the low areas on the ground.

She hoped the clip-clop of the horse's hooves drowned out her pounding heart. His casual way of asking her to stay with his *kinner* felt as if he were courting her and she belonged here on the seat next to him.

She wiped those impossible thoughts out of her head and tried to enjoy the ride to his house. Jacob was waiting for them on the porch when they arrived. He jumped off the last step and ran pell-mell over the grass to reach the buggy when it stopped. Sarah stepped down and into two small arms, which hugged her around the waist.

He stepped back. "Sarah, can you stay all night?"

"*Nein*, Jacob. I'll be back before evening and take Sarah home. You must entertain her while I'm gone. Show her all the things we missed the last time she was on the farm."

"*Jah*, Daed. We'll have a *gut* time."

"I brought you and your sister some cookies from the bakery." She handed him the sack. "Please take them into the house." He ran up the porch steps and into the house, letting the door bang shut.

"I'll try to be back before dark, but if I'm not, don't worry. My driver can take you home."

"I'll pray for your *bruder*."

Just then, a car pulled into the drive and stopped. "He's early." Caleb waved at the driver, hurried to unhook Snowball, said goodbye and climbed into the car. His face looked pale and fear pooled in his eyes. She knew that feeling well, as memories of Samuel's accident came flooding back to her. She could still recall her *ehemann* lying on the ground after his horse bucked him off, his skull crushed on a rock. The only thing she could do was sit in a chair next to his bed and watch him slowly die. She prayed Caleb wouldn't have to go through that with his *bruder*.

She'd stay as long as Caleb needed her to watch his *kinner*. Who could find fault with that?

Jacob came running out of the *haus* and skidded to a stop. "They're in the cookie jar."

Sarah tousled Jacob's hair. "So, what should we do today?"

Jacob's mouth broadened with a smile. "I'm going to take you to see Tiger first. I want you to see how much he has grown."

"Okay. Just let me see if Mary needs my help

with anything." She found her on the back porch, folding laundry. Sarah picked up a towel and took a whiff. "Mmm, I love the fresh, outdoorsy fragrance of laundry when it's hung in the sunshine."

Mary wrinkled her nose.

Sarah folded the towel and laid it on the pile. "Do you need help folding or help with anything else?"

Mary looked up and rolled her eyes, with no attempt at hiding her rude expression. "Ah, *nein*. I can do it. You didn't need to come. I told Daed I could handle this. I do everything when Daed's out in the field, including all his chores."

"I'm sure your *daed*'s just worried since he wouldn't be close and wanted an adult here."

Mary rolled her eyes again and huffed.

Sarah turned to leave, but Mary clearing her voice made her turn back around.

"Later, would you show me how to make Daed's favorite dishes, Rouladen and Black Forest cake?"

Sarah smiled. "Yes. I can do that. I'll go with Jacob for an hour, then come back and help you." She was surprised Mary suddenly needed her help, but at least it was a start.

Jacob escorted her across the barnyard, toward the barn. The breeze whipped her untied *kapp* strings around, pulling a few strands of hair loose from her bun. She straightened the *kapp* and tucked the wisps behind her ear.

Horse's hooves and buggy wheels on the road grabbed her attention. What if someone saw her here and told the bishop? Jacob took off running ahead of her, calling for his cat. Sarah hurried behind him, hoping to reach the barn before anyone saw her.

Jacob pulled the squeaky barn door open, then waited for her. When she grabbed the door, he ran in.

"Here, Tiger."

Sarah heard meowing.

Jacob disappeared behind a stall door and, five seconds later, jumped out, holding Tiger in front of him.

Sarah squealed. "Oh, he's grown so big. You must be feeding him well."

"*Jah.* He's a *gut* mouser, too. Do you want to hold him?"

"Ah, well, he's quite big. Why don't you just set him down, and I can watch him?"

Jacob lowered Tiger to the floor. Immediately the cat's ears perked up. His nose began twitching; he took a crouched position and crept along the floor so quietly, Sarah couldn't even hear him move. He rounded the corner and disappeared back into the barn.

"Tiger's probably on the scent of a mouse. I'll

show you the garden, and then I have a surprise for you at the pond."

"Okay. But after that, I promised to help Mary make a new dish for supper."

They walked out into the barnyard. The garden was spread along the drive and back behind the house. Her eyes roamed over the rows of vegetables and the strawberry patch. "Your garden looks great, Jacob. *Nein* weeds. And your tomatoes are so tall."

"We started the tomatoes in the house in January. I watered them."

"They are very nice plants. *Gut* job."

"Come on. I have a surprise for you at the pond." Jacob hurried down to the edge of the water and pointed to the middle of the pond.

"Is that a duck?" she asked.

"*Jah.* She comes every year and Daed floats a nest for her to lay her eggs in. He said if I watch her closely, a few hours after the ducklings hatch, she'll walk them to the English River, where they'll be safe from predators."

"What a *wonderbaar* surprise. Now I need to get back to the house to help your sister make supper." As she turned to leave, a buggy passed by on the road. She didn't see the driver's face, but he might have noticed her.

"I'll walk you back and then play with Tiger in the yard."

Sarah hurried to the *haus*, washed her hands and looked over the chuck roast Mary had cut into ten strips for the Rouladen. "You'll need to pound the meat to a quarter of an inch. I'll write down the recipes for the meat filling and the Black Forest cake."

Mary made the filling and spread it onto the strips, rolled the meat tightly into cylindrical shapes, then tied the bundle with twine and browned them. When done, she layered them in a Dutch oven to simmer until supper. Mary bent over the pot. "Mmm, it smells *gut*." She looked at Sarah and smiled. "I'm ready to start the cake."

Sarah handed Mary the recipe and helped her gather the ingredients. Then she watched as Mary made the cake and the filling. She topped it with whipped cream, cherries and chocolate shavings.

Sarah took a step closer and twirled the platter holding the cake. "Any bakery would *liebe* to have this in their display case to sell. It looks perfect."

Mary's face beamed. *"Danki."*

Sarah stacked the dirty dishes and carried them to the sink. Mary scooted ahead and stood in front of the sink. "I'll take care of the cleanup, Sarah. It's my supper. I want to do it all. You can talk to

Jacob. I'm sure he's got something else to show you."

"I'd like to help you. It would take half the time with both of us working."

"I'll take care of it."

Jah, at least they got along for a little while, Sarah thought as she left the kitchen.

She wandered out to the barnyard, sat on the grass and watched Jacob play with his cat. He held a piece of twine and pulled it over the grass, and Tiger chased it around. They ran back and forth across the yard until Jacob ran to the garden and back.

"You two make me tired just watching you." Sarah patted the grass.

Jacob flopped onto the ground next to her. "I'm tired. Let's rest, Tiger." He told her about planting and hoeing the garden and what a big help he was.

The dinner bell rang at 7:00 p.m. Sarah sprang to her feet. "Your *daed* must be home. Let's hurry and see how your *onkel* is doing. I'll race you to the *haus*. One, two, three, go!"

Jacob outran her, continued up the porch steps and held the door open.

"You beat me." She panted as she entered the kitchen and looked around. "Is your *daed* here, Mary?"

"*Nein*. Since he was worried about Onkel Peter,

he might stay late at the hospital. We'll eat without him."

"I'm sorry he didn't make it home to try your dinner."

"The leftovers will still taste *gut*. Sit. I'll say the prayer since Daed's not here."

It seemed strange to sit and eat without Caleb's presence at the head of the table. Sarah filled her plate and tried the Rouladen. "Mmm. It's delicious. *Gut* job, Mary."

Mary's face glowed with pride.

Sarah cleared the table and wouldn't take *nein* from Mary this time. She planted her feet in front of the sink and stayed there, helping Mary wash dishes until the last one was placed in the cupboard.

Sarah wandered to the sitting room, sat in the wooden rocker and relaxed. She hadn't expected Caleb to stay so late at the hospital. Maybe his *bruder* had gotten worse.

She pulled her mending out of her bag and worked for an hour on repairing a frayed seam in an apron. She examined her stitches, then tucked it back in the bag.

At nine o'clock the *kinner* stepped into the sitting room smelling all clean with a lavender soap scent lingering on their hands "*Gut nacht*, Sarah." They chirped in unison.

"Sweet dreams, *kinner*." As their footfalls

drummed on the stairs, their hushed voices but distinguishable words floated back to Sarah.

"Why did you ask Sarah to help you with supper? Thought you didn't like her?"

"It's a *gut* thing you're not a snitch or I wouldn't tell you. 'Cause if I can cook well, Daed won't need to get married."

Stunned, Sarah stopped the motion of the rocking chair. Mary's words washed over her like a tidal wave. It wasn't going to be easy to win her over, if she ever could.

Sarah turned the lantern up, steadied the chair with her hands on the armrests and rose from the rocker. She strolled around the room. A quilt stand stood against the wall with two quilts laying over it. One had a double wedding ring pattern in green colors and the other had autumn-colored leaves set in blocks. The needlework stitching looked perfect.

Some handiwork that didn't look finished sat in a sewing basket. The basket had blue fabric covering the lid, and underneath the fabric was cotton stuffing to make it a pincushion. A handle attached to the lid had *Martha* stitched across it. Sarah wandered back to the rocking chair and pulled a well-worn Bible off the end table. She noticed the inscription on the first page. *Presented to Martha Brenneman.*

Sarah pressed a hand to her chin. Martha's

memory remained very much alive in this house. Her heart skipped a beat as her eyes took another quick survey around. Was Caleb ready to remarry? A smidgen of dread wrapped around her middle and inched its way to her throat. She turned the lantern out, sat in the rocker, laid her head back and closed her eyes.

"Wake up, Sarah."

A voice penetrated her hazy head. "What?" She opened her eyes slowly as she tried to erase the trailing effects of sleep.

Caleb stood before her, still wearing his coat.

"How is your *bruder*?" She stretched and sat up.

"He finally came out of the coma and is doing better. He's going to be okay."

"That's *wunderbaar* news, Caleb." She stood and smoothed the winkles out of her dress. "What time is it?"

"It's 4:00 a.m."

"What! I've been here all night. I need to get to the bakery. I should be starting the baking right now." She grabbed her bag.

"The driver is still here and will take you to Kalona."

"I didn't plan on staying the whole night at your home." Panic swept through her.

"I'm sorry, Sarah. No one will know." His annoyingly calm voice did not reassure her.

If the bishop found out, who knows what would happen to her this time. Her knees shook as she closed the car door.

The bishop might even ask her to explain her behavior, or worse, to confess on bended knee in front of the entire church.

Fear prickled the hair on her arms. Next Sunday, she could be facing community discipline.

Would they accept her explanation and give her a pardon?

Chapter Seven

Sarah slumped against the bakery's counter. Staying with Caleb's *kinner* until 4:00 a.m. had drained her. She inhaled a deep whiff of lemon bars, chocolate cake and a medley of pastries that assailed her senses. Even the sugary-sweet smell made her sluggish this morning.

She glanced at the clock, pushed away from the counter, meandered to the front door and turned the sign to Open. Tuesday was normally a slow day, and she hoped today was no exception. The steamy aroma of freshly brewed coffee wafted in her face as she came back around the counter.

Ach. A cup of medium-roast would perk her right up. Her hands cradled the cup as she sipped the rich black liquid. "Mmm."

The doorbell jingled. She turned and faced Elder Abraham Glick. "*Gut* mornin', Abraham. What can I get you?" She set her cup out of the way.

"If you have a minute, I'd like to talk with you."

Abraham had been her *daed*'s best friend and a man whom she'd more than once trusted with a secret. Like the time she skipped school to go fishing and he caught her at the pond. He said he wouldn't tell her *daed*. He didn't, but instead convinced her to confess.

"Would you like a cup of coffee and a cinnamon roll? It's on the house."

"Just coffee."

She set the cup in front of Abraham and sat opposite him. "What's this about, Abe?"

"Yesterday, I went past Caleb Brenneman's farm and saw you in the yard with his *bu*."

She drew in a deep breath. "Caleb's *bruder* was critically injured and in the hospital in a coma. He wanted to stay with him and asked me to watch his *kinner*."

"Sarah, the bishop warned you. I know Alvin's not at the top of your list of men to marry. But you need to avoid Caleb Brenneman. He's New Order, and nothing can come of it but trouble."

Her cheeks burned as she caught a hint of judgment in Abe's voice. "That's why watching Caleb's *kinner* shouldn't make any difference. I do not plan to leave my church, nor do I want disciplining. But I will help a friend in need, especially in an emergency."

Abe shrugged. "You don't want Bishop Yoder

discovering you disobeyed his warning. If others know you went to his farm unescorted, they'll talk. Then you'll have to confess. I'm here as your friend, Sarah. Take care."

"*Danki*, Abraham, for stopping by." Sarah walked him to the door, unshed tears blurring her vision. She wasn't sorry she'd helped Caleb, but she was sorry for the chaos her actions had created for friends like Abraham when they were put into the difficult place of keeping a secret. Abe even took a chance by warning her. The bishop would expect Abe to report her.

All day she worked alongside Hannah in the kitchen as much as possible, trying to keep from watching and waiting for a visit from the bishop. Abraham's warning spun around in her head. She wasn't a child. She wasn't skipping work to go fishing. It had been an emergency, helping Caleb and his *kinner*.

Sarah glanced at the clock. One hour until closing.

A breeze swirled through the shop and a commotion at the door pulled Sarah's attention from cleaning the counter. Caleb and Jacob heaved a large toolbox over the threshold and plunked it on the floor. She propped her hands on her hips. "What are you two up to?"

"You helped me out while I was at the hospital, and I wanted to repay the debt. We are here to do repairs in the kitchen. Should only take an hour or so. I brought a helper."

"*Jah*, I see that." She surveyed the *bu*'s attire.

Jacob patted his tool belt, which drooped on one side while his other hand held it up at his waist. He pulled out a tack hammer and held it up. "I'm going to do a lot of work for you today."

"Then it's a *gut* thing you've come dressed like a carpenter. Follow me and you can get started."

"Sarah, before I forget. Mary was wondering if you could show her how to make strawberry jam." Caleb grabbed his toolbox and fell in line behind his *sohn* as they made their way to the kitchen.

"*Jah*, for sure and for certain, I can do that sometime." She watched as they started removing cupboard doors to replace the worn and loose hinges.

Hannah stepped to the sink and pointed to the faucet. "Can you fix this leak?"

Caleb examined the faucet, furrowed his brow and nodded.

Sarah showed Caleb where to place the new towel holder and ceiling saucepan rack, which she had stashed in the closet a month ago.

She ducked out of the kitchen and returned to the front to finish cleaning. After emptying the display case, she set the sheet pan of leftover baked goods in the cooler, then cleaned and sanitized the case like she did every night.

When she glanced in the kitchen and saw the faucet was fixed, she got the impression Hannah wasn't letting the guys leave until all the repairs were completed. She also noticed her friend had a pastry tray waiting on a table for them.

Sarah turned off the coffee pot just before closing and cleaned it. When the bakery was empty, Caleb and Jacob took a break and came to the front of the shop for their treat.

Caleb held up his brownie. "These are *gut*. So are the lemon bars."

Jacob nodded.

Sarah grabbed a napkin and wiped chocolate off one side of Jacob's mouth and lemon off the other side. The enticement was too great. She snatched a brownie off the tray and popped it into her mouth. When the doorbell jingled, she turned in time to see the bishop enter.

She cringed as she met him at the counter. "What can I help you with, Bishop Yoder? We are about to close."

"I wanted to talk with you, Sarah." He glanced at the table area.

"I'm having repairs done in the kitchen." She gestured toward the back. "The repairmen are here now. Could we do it another time, say tomorrow?"

"*Jah*, I guess it will wait until then." He scowled at her as he walked out.

Sarah followed him to the door, turned the dead bolt and flipped the sign to Closed.

As she headed back to the table, a knock sounded on the door.

Startled, she slowly twisted around. She blew out a long breath and ran to the door. "Bertha, we're closed."

"*Jah*, but I was wondering if I could give you a special order for tomorrow."

"Of course. Come in." Sarah took the order, ushered Bertha out and locked back up while Caleb and Jacob returned to the kitchen. She gazed out over the near-empty street, anxiety washing over her. The bishop's visit flashed back to her. What could he want? Had he too found out about her going to Caleb's farm? Helping someone in need *was not* wrong. So why did her insides whisper something different?

She glanced toward the kitchen, where Caleb and Jacob were finishing their work. Would the bishop make her choose between the Brennemans and her faith? A dread wrapped around her heart.

Sarah had a mess to clean up, and she didn't mean just the kitchen. Before meeting with the bishop, she had to decide what mattered most: Caleb and his family, or her faith and her family…

She let out a deep sigh. They were only friends.

Why did she have to give them up? *Jah*, she knew the bishop was afraid her friendship with Caleb would turn into something more.

The thing was…she was afraid it wouldn't.

If she chose her faith and her family, it meant life without Caleb and Jacob. She couldn't choose Caleb and leave her church or she'd be shunned.

Hannah entered the room brushing her hands over her apron. "What did the bishop want?"

"To talk to me. He noticed Caleb and Jacob were here and decided to wait until tomorrow."

Hannah glanced back at the open kitchen door and whispered. "Think he knows you went out to the farm and watched the *kinner*?"

"I'm sure he's heard a story embellished by people who think they know what's what. Two buggies went by while I was outside at the farm."

"I have some news to tell you before someone else does." Hannah wrapped an arm around her friend's shoulder.

Sarah's back stiffened. "What else are they dishing out about me? Your tone is scaring me."

"Sorry. It isn't bad news. Well, maybe bad for me, but *gut* for your *bruder*. I heard Turner has been seeing Naomi Flickinger."

Sarah gasped. "I can't believe he didn't tell me. Courting is supposed to be secret, but I'm his sister." Sarah pressed a hand to her heart. "*Nein*. I don't believe that."

"Who knows? Maybe it's not true," Hannah said. "Maybe he's making her cupboards or hanging new doors."

"*Jah*. We'll see. They could be talking about Turner like they do me. The gossips need someone to wag their tongues about since it's a small town and they have nothing else to do."

"What are you going to say when the bishop comes back? Have you decided?" Worry threaded through each of Hannah's words.

Sarah froze. "I've delayed making the decision, hoping it'd take care of itself."

"Oh, Sarah." Hannah folded her friend into a hug and held her there for several minutes. "If the bishop decides upon discipline, and you don't confess, the Amish won't come to the bakery."

"I know, but we get hundreds of tourists, at least during seven months of the year, and maybe longer if it's not too cold during the holidays. I'm praying for a long tourist season so I can save enough money for the winter months."

"You know…if you're shunned, I can't work here." Hannah's voice quaked.

Silence stretched out between them. "*Jah*. I was trying not to think about it. The man is Amish. So why should it be such a big deal?"

"He's New Order, and a lot of what they believe is against our *Ordnung*," Hannah whispered.

"I'm not marrying Alvin. I just can't." Tears

clouded her vision. She blinked them back. "Why should they bully me with something so important? It's as if they're not thinking of my needs, only his. I know our faith believes we must give of ourselves to our community, but not my whole life."

Sarah never thought it would go this far. Never thought she'd see Caleb again. Blindly she hoped Alvin would give up.

Caleb's footsteps echoed over the flooring as he stepped to the side to maneuver his toolbox through the kitchen doorway. As he walked toward the front of the bakery, his tools clanked in the toolbox.

Hannah wrapped an arm around Sarah's shoulders and squeezed. "I'll go talk to Jacob and finish in the kitchen so we can go."

Caleb wore a confident smile. "All done. The cupboard doors are now solid. The racks are up, and we work cheap. A dessert should finish the payment."

"Okay, but I owe you more than that, Caleb."

"*Nein.* You were at the house all day and night with my *kinner.*"

Jah, and Abraham would never let her forget it…unless she confessed.

The question was, would the bishop forget it if she confessed? Or would he insist she marry Alvin?

* * *

Caleb stood so close to Sarah, he could reach out and touch her. *Nein.* Pull her into his arms and press a kiss to her lips. Sweat beaded on his forehead. He set his toolbox on the bakery floor and blotted his brow with his shirtsleeve.

His tongue felt like dried shoe leather with Sarah so near. He wasn't sure he could even form a word. He raised his gaze from her lips to her eyes.

Sarah's voice hitched a bit. "I set the desserts in the cooler in the kitchen. You can take your pick."

Caleb followed Sarah to the cooler and let a cool blast of air hit him. He drew in a deep breath. "What I'd really like for my dessert is to go on a picnic with you Sunday afternoon."

She smiled at him. "Do you want me to bring the dessert then, or will you take it now?"

"Bring it to the picnic. Jacob and I will fetch you early Sunday morning so you can attend Sunday school with us."

"I'll be ready." A blush rose to her cheeks, but it made her look even more fetching to Caleb.

Sarah locked the bakery door and hurried to catch Turner at his woodworking shop. As she drew closer, a faint light was visible in the back of his building. She knocked on the side door and tried the handle.

Locked.

She knocked harder. He lived in the back, and the light was on, so he should be there. Maybe he'd stepped out?

She tapped louder.

Faint footsteps came toward the door, and then it opened. "Sarah, what are you doing here?" Turner's voice sounded surprised.

"If you have a few minutes, I need to talk with you."

"If it's about repairs, I'm working on a big order, so I can't do them right away."

"*Nein.* A friend did the repairs. Can I come in a minute?" Turner stood in front of the doorway, as if he were too busy to see her.

"For a minute. I'm still working in the shop." He stepped back.

"Bishop Yoder is pestering me about marrying Alvin Studer. I don't want to marry Alvin. I heard he hit his late *frau*."

"Don't believe that. Alvin is a quiet man. A hard worker. He owns a large farm and hires many youngies to help him work it. He'll make you a *gut ehemann*. Stop worrying. You won't need to run the bakery anymore."

She gasped. "I *liebe* the bakery. I don't plan to quit working there."

"What are you here for then?" His abruptness cut her off. He huffed so hard, it stirred the hair at her temples.

"The bishop stopped by before closing, but with so many still at the bakery, I told him to come back tomorrow. You should know, when Caleb Brenneman's *bruder* was in an accident and in a coma, I went to his farm and watched his *kinner* while he went to the hospital and sat with his sister-in-law and *bruder*. I think Bishop Yoder either wants to discipline me or wants me to marry Alvin. I want you to tell the bishop that I'm not going to marry Alvin."

Turner squinted at her against the darkened hallway. He lowered his chin and focused back on her. "Alvin is a decent man. He's in our Order, and Caleb Brenneman is not. You should help people in your own district and let Caleb's church help his family."

Sarah stepped back. She couldn't believe he had said that. He was as strict as Daed. Daed had insisted she marry Samuel but she hadn't minded. He was a *gut* man, a fair man, but a typical strict Amish man.

"I will not talk to the bishop for you, Sarah. Get that out of your head. I warned you about your actions. Now you must deal with the consequences."

She opened the door, slipped through and closed the door behind her. When they were *kinner*, Turner had always stood up for her.

Apparently not anymore.

Chapter Eight

Sarah carefully turned the bakery sign to Open and glanced up the street to see if the bishop was heading in this direction. Ominous dark clouds hung overhead and a cold April drizzle coated the lamppost. It looked black and sinister as it covered the sidewalk and street.

She craned her neck. No one was out driving yet. Maybe the inclement weather would force the bishop to cancel his visit.

Sarah poured herself a mug of coffee, took a sip and checked the front window. She jerked back, almost spilling the hot brew. The bishop had parked his buggy and was heading toward the bakery door.

He slipped off his coat and hat and hung them on a hook. He motioned to a table. "Sarah, join me."

She gulped a mouthful of coffee, dribbling a

few drops out the corner of her parted lips and down her chin. She grabbed a napkin and blotted the moisture. Her body reluctantly moved, like the time Daed had asked her to pull a switch from a tree so he could discipline her.

She poured the bishop a cup of medium-roast, hoping it would help soften his mood. "Bishop Yoder, I wasn't sure anyone would risk the streets today." She set the cup in front of him. "Haven't had any customers, but I have plenty of coffee."

He glared at her as she sat opposite him. "Alvin should be here soon."

His words knocked the wind out of her. She dragged in a ragged breath and tried to calm her racing pulse.

The bishop reached out with his fingertips and tapped the table twice. "We live our lives for Jesus Christ. As Christ gave up his life for us, we too must sacrifice. We must yield our will to *Gott*'s will."

Jah, she understood that, but how did the bishop know that *Gott* wanted her to marry Alvin?

The bishop straightened his back. "To be part of the church district means we must give up what is personal and selfish. We live in a community and give of ourselves to that community."

She gulped. "Bishop Yoder, I don't want to be Alvin's wife. *Ever.*"

"You don't believe in community?"

"Of course I do. I work at church events and at barn raisings. When someone is sick or injured, I help."

"Jah." He nodded. "I understand. You just need to spend time with Alvin because you do not know him well enough. That is perfectly normal. Get to know him and his *kinner.* You'll feel differently."

Sarah stared at the bishop in disbelief. *He's insisting I court Alvin!*

The bakery door opened and out of the corner of her eye, she could see a man enter. Her heart raced.

Alvin.

Her whole body went numb as Alvin slipped around behind her.

He pulled out the chair on her left. *"Gut* mornin', Sarah." The words fell off his silky tongue.

"Jah." It was the only word she could form out of her mouth.

"Alvin was wondering if you would grant him permission to court you," the bishop blurted out.

She was stunned. How could she reply to that? Did she disobey the bishop and not give Alvin a chance?

Daggers stabbed at her heart as she slouched against the back of the chair. If she courted Alvin, she couldn't see Caleb and his family again.

The door banged open and Bertha Bontrager burst through like a bulldozer. She removed her bonnet and hung it on the coatrack. "It's not fit for car or buggy this morning." She laughed.

"Mornin', Bertha. I thought maybe you'd pick up your order later today or tomorrow with the weather so bad." Sarah rose from the table and nodded at the bishop. "I'll just be a minute."

Sarah pointed toward the kitchen. "Your order is in the back."

"No hurry."

When she returned to the front of the bakery, Bertha was sitting at the table with Alvin and the bishop. She sat the order on the table. "Coffee, Bertha?"

"*Jah.* And a cinnamon-swirl roll, please."

Sarah took her time pouring the coffee. There was one large swirl, the last one made. She had been planning to save it for a male customer that came in, but it'd take a woman a while to eat.

Sarah slid the cinnamon swirl on a plate and placed it and a cup of coffee in front of Bertha while she listened to her describing the slick and dangerous conditions of the road coming into town. Brushing off the temptation to disappear back into the kitchen, Sarah silently prayed Bertha would stay as long as Alvin did.

Fifteen minutes later, Melinda Miller bumped the door open with her hip. She held her *boppli* in her arms and tried to keep the blowing rain off their faces while she maneuvered over the threshold.

Danki, Lord. Sarah stood and rushed to help Melinda.

The bishop pushed his chair back, scraping the floor with its wooden legs, tipped his hat to Sarah and headed out the door.

"Have a nice day, Bishop Yoder." Sarah almost sang the words but reined in her glee.

As Alvin pushed back his chair, Bertha stood with him. "Later today, I'll bring a casserole by for those six *kinner* of yours."

Alvin smiled and nodded. "*Danki*, Bertha."

After the bakery was empty, Hannah stepped out front. "Go on a buggy ride with Alvin and explain how you feel. Tell him you're still in love with Samuel."

"*Jah*, like that's going to stop him. He has six reasons and a houseful of work not to care what I think. He might not care if I like him or not."

Caleb's heart galloped when Sarah sat next to him. The buggy swayed as it hit a bump, and he hoped it would move her closer. He liked the feel of her sitting next to him.

When they arrived, he introduced Sarah to everyone at Sunday school. The women had brought breakfast casseroles, biscuits and jam to eat before they started their Bible study. Sarah mingled with the women. She knew most of them, probably from the bakery. Sarah expressed an interest in learning about assurance of salvation, something the Old Order didn't view as necessary, and he hoped she would keep coming back to Bible study. Maybe it would persuade her to join his church.

Yet if his *tochter* didn't accept Sarah, he wasn't sure what he'd do. He wanted his *kinner* to like the woman he might choose as his *frau*. He'd wait until after the picnic with his *kinner* to get Mary's reaction.

He leaned closer to Sarah as he shared his lesson book and Bible with her. She smelled of lilacs and springtime. She read scripture and discussed it with the group. She listened to the others and contributed from her experience. Her faith was sound and he could tell she had a deep *liebe* for *Gott*. When they stood to leave, everyone invited her to come back again.

Deep inside Caleb, tiny sprouts of feelings for her had blossomed.

Sarah tilted her head back and let the sunbeams shower her with warmth. The *kinner* were excited about the picnic. Mary acted less sulky and even chatted with her the whole time they laid out the picnic. It wasn't much, but she hoped it was a start to friendship.

When the picnic was over, Sarah hurried to wrap the food and place it in the basket while Caleb and the *kinner* set up the volleyball net. "Girls against guys," she yelled out.

"Jah," Caleb grinned. "If the girls lose, they have to make the guys their favorite meal with dessert."

Jacob squealed. "We are going to win, Daed."

"Okay," Mary chimed in. "But if the girls win, they get to pick a chore the guys have to do for them."

Caleb nodded in agreement. "Girls can go first."

Sarah served the ball over the net and Caleb returned it. Back and forth it went. First one team scored a point, then the other.

"You hit like an old man, Jacob," Mary teased.

"I do not." Jacob smacked the ball with all his energy and watched it sail over Mary's head to win the guys a point and the game.

Sarah checked the time. "I've had a great afternoon, but I need to get home. Pick a day this week, and Mary and I will make dinner."

On the way home, Sarah stole glances at Caleb, while his attention focused on maneuvering the buggy along the rough road. He had his straw hat pulled low over his forehead, shading his square jaw and powerful chin. His beard looked freshly trimmed and attractive. Her heart nearly skipped a beat.

Caleb talked to her about the farm and the progress of his crops. "They should yield a nice profit." Sarah nodded at his announcement. She smiled at the notion that they acted like a married couple.

When he pulled the buggy to a stop at the back of the bakery, she stepped out, foreboding churning in her stomach. If the bishop threatened her with discipline, she might not be able to see Caleb and his family again. And just when Mary seemed to be warming up to her...

The next Sunday, Sarah sat on the bench after the preaching, waiting for the publishing of the banns and the public announcements.

The preacher glanced from side to side at the filled benches. "I have a joyous announcement to make. Turner Lapp and Naomi Flickinger will be married in two weeks."

Sarah grabbed Hannah's hand and noticed a tear roll down her friend's cheek. "I'm fine, Sarah," Hannah whispered, as she flicked the moisture off her chin.

After the meal, Sarah dropped Hannah off at home and then proceeded to her apartment. Maybe Turner would stop by to invite her to the wedding, as was the custom after the announcement in church. No doubt, they planned a small wedding since they'd both been married before. Finally at 8:00 p.m., she couldn't wait for Turner any longer. She blew out the lamp and tucked herself in for the night.

On Monday morning, Sarah waited as Noah Mullet, Naomi's *bruder*, and two other men placed their morning orders at the bakery counter. One by one, each man took his sweet roll and coffee and sat at a table. When the shop had cleared of patrons, Noah called out, "Sarah, come over here and sit a while. Your *bruder* will be here any minute."

Sarah could feel tension, excitement or something brewing with these men. Were they going to play a joke on her *bruder*? The men had all been friends with Turner for a long time, and often in school had included her in their pranks. What could they possibly be up to? She sat next to Noah. "What's going on? You guys look like you are going to play a joke on someone." When the bakery door burst open, the words caught in her throat.

Turner hurried in and pulled up a chair. "Taking a break, sis?"

"*Jah.* Noah asked me to join them. Sorry if I'm intruding on a *buwe* thing." She started to stand.

"Ah, come on, Sarah, stay and talk." The guys at the table coaxed.

"*Jah*, you're not intruding." Noah waved his hand in a motion for the others to quiet down. "Turner, have you told Sarah your surprise?"

Turner shot Noah a frown. "Sis." His voice shook. He started poking at a crumb on the table, until he slowly brushed it over the table's edge.

"What is it?" He was making her nervous.

Then he let out a hoot. "Naomi and I would like you to help at the wedding, and she would like you to spend the night and get to know her family."

Sarah let the requests soak in. She felt like a traitor to Hannah, but Naomi was going to be her sister-in-law. Of course she would have liked it better if he'd picked Hannah for his *frau*. But she knew that would never happen. "*Jah*, of course I'll help. Whatever Naomi wants me to do. I wish you had told me you were getting married. It seems others knew it before me."

Sarah stood and swept her eyes over the table of men. Guess it was a joke. She was probably the only person in town who didn't suspect her *bruder* was going to marry Naomi. Even after Hannah mentioned it, she didn't want to believe that he wouldn't tell her. Tears welled up in her eyes as she headed for the kitchen. It didn't feel like she and Turner were family any longer.

She grabbed the rolling pin, took the dough she had resting, rolled it flat, scooped up the piecrust and lined a pie dish. She glanced at Hannah. "Did you hear?"

"*Jah*. Now you will have a sister."

"You'll always be my sister, Hannah." Sarah heard heavy footsteps approaching the kitchen doorway. Turner slowly walked to her work area.

"I'll go out and watch the front," Hannah said. "Turner, I'd love to help Naomi family's get ready for the wedding, too."

"*Danki*, Hannah. That would be nice." He waited until Hannah had left the kitchen. "Sarah, why did you run off like that?"

Her heart pounding like a blacksmith's hammer, she laid a hand on her chest as if to stop the banging sound that echoed from her chest to her ears. "Turner, everyone in town knew but me. Why the secrecy? You couldn't tell me?"

"Once I get married and we start a family, I won't have much time to help do repairs at the bakery. I was hoping you'd marry Alvin, then I wouldn't have to worry. But you seemed so against Alvin, I didn't know how to approach it with you. As it is, I'm trying to save money, working every waking minute and taking extra orders. You should think about marrying Alvin so you will have someone to take care of you."

"I see. Someone to take care of me. Alvin has

a big farm with hired help, six *kinner* that need caring for with lots of dirty laundry and meals that need cooking, but *I* am the one who needs taking care of!" She turned back to her pie. "Get out of here, Turner, and leave me alone."

Sarah trotted to the stove and stirred the pan of rhubarb that was simmering for the pie. Like the wispy plume of steam rising from the fruit, silence filled the air.

"You're a stubborn woman, sister."

Turner's footsteps trailed off as he headed to the front of the shop. Sarah dropped to her knees and prayed. She took a long look at the height, breadth and depth of her problem, and knew what she had to do.

Chapter Nine

Sarah woke in a sweat and gasped. It was Turner's wedding day. A shiver of fear swept over her heart. She'd have to dodge the bishop and Alvin all day. What if the bishop acting as Alvin's *Schtecklimann*—go-between—tried to corner her to set a wedding date? *Ach*, she'd have to avoid them, or give a firm *nein*.

She pushed herself out of bed and slipped into her dress. She'd promised to help her sister-in-law-to-be get ready for the wedding.

It was time her *bruder* remarried. His *frau* had died several years ago. In school, he'd teased Naomi, but when they started to go to singings, Ethan had asked first to take Naomi home and Turner had lost his chance. Sarah remembered how he'd moped for months, until he met his late *frau*. Now he'd have a second chance at happiness with Naomi.

Sarah placed the wedding cake she'd made in the buggy, hitched her horse, King, and stopped on the way to pick up her friend. "How are you doing, Hannah?"

"I'm telling myself that Turner is my *bruder* and I must be happy for him and Naomi." Hannah settled herself in the seat and set her cake on her lap. Her cake would be only one of many decorated cakes baked by close friends.

She reached over and gave Hannah's hand a quick squeeze. Sarah swallowed the lump in her throat, shook King's reins and changed the subject. She pointed out yards with beautiful tulips, daffodils, snowball trees in bloom and bushes with bright red leaves.

While Sarah turned the buggy slowly into the driveway, Hannah braced the cakes with her hands. Naomi's *daed* ran over, helped them down and then climbed into the buggy to hand them the cakes.

Sarah led the way to the living room, which was cleared of furniture, and set her cake on an *Eck* table—V-shaped tables, placed in the corner for the bridal party. Hannah hesitantly set hers down, too. Sarah glanced at her friend and noticed tears shimmering in her eyes.

"I'm so sorry, Hannah. I know how this must hurt."

She drew a deep breath. "I'm fine." Her voice

shook a little as she swiped her hands down her apron as if fighting for composure.

"Come on." Sarah patted Hannah on the shoulder. "Let's help in the kitchen until it's time for the wedding. That'll keep our minds busy."

Sarah helped prepare food and made sure the tables were set and the breads were sliced. At 9:00 a.m., the bridal party were already in their places and the singing had begun.

At the ceremony, Sarah watched the happy couple. Naomi looked *wunderbaar* in her new green dress that brought out the specks of jade in her hazel eyes. Turner gazed at Naomi with admiration, and joy radiated from her face. They made *liebe* look easy, Sarah decided. If only her *liebe* life were as simple as theirs appeared.

After dinner, Sarah slipped off to the kitchen to help with cleanup and keep out of Alvin's sight. When she ventured to the living room to clear tables, Alvin called her name, but she pretended she didn't hear and dashed back to the kitchen, carrying plates.

In the late afternoon, Sarah watched the happy couple visit with their guests. Naomi ran over to Sarah, hugged her and whispered, "*Danki* for helping, sister-in-law."

"You're welcome. I'm happy for both of you." Sarah gave each of them a kiss on the cheek when Turner strolled over to them.

"Your wedding is next, *jah*? Then I can help you." Naomi's eyes crinkled with excitement.

"It won't be anytime soon." Sarah shot Turner a smirk.

He turned back to his *frau*. "We need to see other guests."

Sarah picked up empty cake plates and stacked them until her hands were full. The pile teetered and tipped toward her a little too much until they dumped crumbs on her apron. She set the stack on a table, pulled her apron away from her dress and brushed the crumbs onto a plate. Sarah noticed a man approaching and looked up into Alvin's smiling face.

Ach—caught.

Laying her shaking and soiled hands on her apron, Sarah glanced into his eyes and their unnerving glint. She flashed a smile. "There you are, Alvin. I was wondering when I'd see you. I've promised Naomi and her *mamm* I'd stay here tonight to help with the cleanup and to get better acquainted with my extended family."

"*Jah*, I understand." The glint disappeared from Alvin's eyes and his chest deflated with a sigh. "I'll see you later, Sarah."

She grabbed some leftovers and hurried to the kitchen before he thought of something else to say.

A twinge of regret poked her. *I must tell him soon I'm not going to marry him.*

"I heard that. You lied to him."

Sarah whipped around. "No, I didn't, Hannah. They asked, and *jah*, I might stay." She handed Hannah a stack of dirty dishes.

"You need to explain to Alvin how you feel. He's a reasonable man."

"Maybe, but I can't chance it."

Hannah set the empty bowls and platters next to the sink and set glasses and silverware in the sudsy water. She pushed up her sleeves and began washing glasses. "What are you afraid of?"

Sarah glanced at the ceiling and took a few steps closer to Hannah. "That the bishop and Alvin will set a date for the wedding, announce it in church and force me to marry him or leave town. You are a lot more trusting than I am, Hannah. Maybe because you've never been married and had someone make all your decisions for you."

The wood flooring squeaked behind Sarah.

Hannah stopped washing dishes, turned around and gasped. Her eyes darted from someone behind Sarah to Sarah.

Sarah placed a hand on her throat. *It must be Alvin.* Well, at least now he knows, but she didn't mean to hurt his feelings. She pivoted slowly, like a rusty nut on a bolt.

Caleb stood there, holding a tray of dirty glasses and plates. "I saw you dart through the house, picking up dirty dishes, and thought I'd help you out."

Sarah's stomach twisted. "What are you doing here, Caleb?"

"I know Naomi Flickinger's *daed*. He even got me a *gut* deal with Turner on replacing my kitchen-cabinet doors. I've been thinking about sprucing up my house. It's time. I thought I might bump into you here."

"Turner is my *bruder*." Her voice squeaked.

"Ah, with different last names, I had no idea he was kin to you." His voice wavered.

Several women bustled into the kitchen and interrupted Caleb, their arms and hands burdened with dishes and food to store. Sarah searched Caleb's face, his eyes throwing an icy stare toward her.

He nodded and set the tray on the table. "Nice to see you again, Sarah," he said and walked out.

Caleb swallowed hard as he headed out the door. He glanced around at the cloudless deep blue sky. To him, the blue only reflected the bruising of his heart.

His heart pounded against his chest, trying its best to punch its way out. His palms drenched in sweat, he'd almost dropped the glassware. He'd planned to toss out the dirty paper napkins, but all he wanted was to get as far away from Sarah as possible.

So, the beautiful Sarah had an admirer. Alvin. Of course a woman like her, who could pluck a star from the sky, had someone courting her. Most assuredly, Alvin was Old Order, so there was no conflict with church affiliation. He knew that was the biggest problem for him and Sarah to overcome. She didn't want to change churches, and neither did he. He'd thought he could convince her otherwise when he took her to Sunday school and Bible study.

On his way to the buggy, Caleb tried to force a smile to all those he met. It was difficult to do so with a stabbing pain in his gut. Sarah had an obvious attachment to Jacob, and in befriending Caleb, had he mistaken it as affection aimed at him? His face still burned with embarrassment.

"Fool," he mumbled through gritted teeth as he climbed in the buggy. "You're a fool." He pointed Snowball toward home.

He trotted Snowball a little faster than usual for a few miles. He lightly pulled on the reins to slow the horse. "Whoa there, settle down, boy." The steed evidently sensed his agitation. Why should he take things out on his horse because he took a browbeating of his own making?

It was time he stopped daydreaming about Sarah Gingerich and erased this infatuation from his head and heart.

Sarah knocked on the door to Caleb's house.

No answer.

She knocked again.

Silence.

She hadn't seen Alvin or Caleb in a couple of weeks—not since the wedding. Previously both of them had sought her out. Now neither one came around. Of course, summer meant hard work for farmers. Some vegetables planted early would be ready to harvest. She had noticed on the ride to his farm that trucks and wagons from canneries waited for produce. That roadside stands, farm markets and women wanting fruits and vegetables for canning and freezing would be waiting too. Caleb, no doubt, was very busy.

One last knock.

Sarah heard footsteps approaching the door, too light for Caleb, but too heavy for Jacob. The door swung open and Mary stood before her, looking frazzled and nearly worn out.

"Your *daed* told me you'd like to learn how to make jam. It's the perfect time, since strawberries are in season, if you'd like me to show you?"

Mary shrugged.

"Four hands are better than two." Sarah raised her brow.

"Could you show me how to can vegetables, too?" Mary asked.

"*Jah*, be glad to help. Ready to start now, or is another day better?"

Opening the door wider, she allowed Sarah to enter. They tackled the jam first. When they finished with that, Mary pointed to the big pot of string beans waiting in the corner.

"I picked them yesterday. There should be enough for eight quarts." It saved time that Mary had thought to wash and sterilize the jars the day before.

"Do you have much experience with canning, Mary?" She replied that her *mamm*'s sisters had helped. When Mary asked questions to learn, Sarah tried to teach her all she could.

An hour later Mary's tongue had loosened. "Are you and my *daed* courting?" Mary kept her voice even. "He never mentions you anymore."

Out of the mouths of young'ins. Sarah stayed silent, hoping that would signal Mary to drop the subject.

"Are you two still friends?" Sarah couldn't decide by Mary's tone whether she was glad or not.

Apparently she decided Sarah wasn't going to

answer, but Mary was in a mood to talk. "I'm fourteen on my next birthday."

"Oh? Not much longer until sixteen. Are you looking forward to attending your first singing?" Sarah held a jar as Mary filled it with beans.

"I'm a little nervous."

"Is there a special *bu* you have your eye on?"

"*Nein.* When I asked Daed questions, he said I'm too little to worry about it."

"He might not want to see his little girl growing up so fast. Give him time. He'll get used to the idea."

"He and Mamm were so much in *liebe.* I can't imagine why he wouldn't want that for me." She looked at Sarah thoughtfully. "Mamm was a good cook and a loving person. We all missed her terribly at first, snapping at each other and not wanting to touch anything in the house of hers. Then we decided it wasn't what she would have wanted."

Sarah's heart fell. Maybe Caleb wasn't ready to recommit.

"I know what you're going through, Mary. I lost my *mamm*, my *daed* and my *ehemann*, Samuel, all within two years. It's hard to lose loved ones. I felt like I was numb inside for a very long time. Nothing seemed right. Then one day, the grief lessened and I moved on."

"Exactly." Mary held up the spoon dripping

with hot liquid before dumping its content into the jar. "Mamm would have wanted us to get on with our lives. Last week, I finished some sewing she'd started. Before, I didn't have the heart to move her mending, let alone finish it. Suddenly it just seemed like the right time."

Sarah nodded and sensed Mary was getting through the grieving process.

Three hours later, heavy footsteps tromped up the porch stairs. Then stopped. Sarah straightened her back and squared her shoulders. Had Caleb recognized her buggy?

The door opened and Caleb stepped in. *Jah*, he must be surprised to see her. She glanced over and met his gaze.

He nodded and hung his hat on the hook. "What are you doing here?"

Sarah noticed Mary's head jerk. "I helped Mary make jam, as I promised."

"Oh." The word fell flat. He fetched a cold drink of water and took a sandwich that Mary had made a while ago out of the icebox.

"Is Jacob with you? I thought I might see him while I was here."

"He'll be in shortly. He stopped to see how Tiger's kittens were doing."

"Tiger fathered kittens?"

"*Nein*. Tiger is the *mamm*. Jacob named her,

and I never paid any attention." His voice trailed to a whisper.

"Oh. I see."

Caleb set his empty glass down and headed for the door. "*Danki* for helping Mary." He closed the door and tromped down the porch steps.

Sarah had hoped to find some time alone with Caleb to explain about Alvin, something she should have done earlier. But it didn't look like he was in a mood to listen.

Caleb stomped into the barn. "I appreciate Sarah keeping her promise to Mary, but she doesn't need to feel obligated to us," he mumbled.

"Daed, are you talking to me?" Jacob came out of a stall, Tiger following close behind.

"*Nein.* I'm just talking to myself. Sarah is at the house, helping Mary make jam. She wanted to see you."

"*Danki.* Come on, Tiger. Let's take one of your babies to show her. She might want to keep one."

"Jacob, do not pester Sarah to take a kitten if she says *nein.*"

"I won't." Jacob ran out the door and banged it shut.

Caleb shook his head. That *bu.* He grabbed the scythe and sickle, and sharpened their blades until they had a fine edge. Weeds were tall and he needed to get them cut. He took off his hat and wiped his brow with his sleeve. Why had Sarah come to the farm? To help Mary? Maybe she was no longer courting Alvin. Or she could have wanted to talk to him privately, but he didn't wait long enough to find out.

Nein. If she wanted to talk, she could have said something. Although, she did honor his request to help Mary. He should have at least said good-bye. Caleb hurried out the barn, banging the door closed. He saw Sarah heading to her buggy and ran across the barnyard. "Wait. There's something I want to ask you."

Her face brightened as he approached.

"Are you and Alvin courting?" he blurted out.

"What makes you think that?"

"I overheard you and Hannah talking at Naomi and Turner's wedding."

"Then you misunderstood. Our bishop likes to matchmake the widows and widowers. He tried to match Alvin and me. Bishop Yoder thinks we should court, but I have no intention of courting Alvin."

Sarah paused and Caleb noticed she had a strained expression.

"Hannah thinks I should be honest with Alvin and tell him I'm not going to marry him. But I don't want to be alone with Alvin in a buggy to tell him, and it's awkward with others around."

"Has this been going on the whole time we've known each other?"

"Well…not the whole time."

"Didn't you think you needed to be honest with me?" Caleb's voice tightened.

She took a step back, closer to the buggy. "I was hoping to resolve the situation with Alvin before it got out of hand."

"Before it got out of hand? You don't think it's out of hand now? Surely I made my interests known—taking you to my church, on a picnic, and asking you to supper."

"I thought if I ignored Alvin, he'd get discouraged and find someone else. Then I wouldn't have to worry about hurting his feelings."

"And you didn't care about hurting mine?"

"*Nein.* You're twisting my words. I didn't mean that. I was hoping to spare your feelings by not telling you. Apparently that didn't work."

"Sarah, honesty is the basis of any relationship. Without it, relationships fail."

Caleb headed toward the house. He heard Sarah climb into her buggy and click her tongue. "Giddyap, King."

The wheels crunched over the rocks as the buggy and Sarah drove out of his lane and out of his life. When he turned, his heart was beating wildly, and she'd disappeared behind the grove of trees.

What had he done? He didn't want her out of his life. If she had told him about Alvin, would he have believed Alvin meant nothing to her?

Caleb watched as the buggy stirred up dust, then dissolved into nothingness, like his chance for *liebe*.

Chapter Ten

Caleb banged around in the barn, cleaning the stalls with a pitchfork and tossing soiled straw in a manure spreader.

"Meow."

He glanced over at Tiger and her kittens eyeing him as they always did when it was almost time for milking.

"Meow…meow." One complaint after the other.

"Shoo. Get out of the way."

Bracing the pitchfork prongs against an area that had muck stuck to the floor, he pushed hard to loosen the mess. Then he watched spiders and bugs run across the planks and escape through cracks in the boards. Caleb poked, pulled and shoveled the pitchfork along every inch of flooring.

Thoughts of Sarah crept into his mind and whirled through his head. The thing he disliked most wasn't that Sarah hadn't told him about Alvin. It was his reaction. It made him jealous to think another man pushed so hard to get her. All this time, he'd taken it slow so Mary and Jacob could get to know her. Of course Alvin wanted her for his *frau*. She was beautiful, kind, good with *kinner* and a great cook. Who could ask for anyone more perfect?

Sarah burrowed into his mind and his dreams, and disrupted his work. She mentally tagged around with him every hour of every day. He walked over to the wall and hung the pitchfork and shovel on their hooks. Then he headed toward the house.

His gut twisted in turmoil. Had he sent her away, into the waiting arms of Alvin? His heart cringed with each step he took. *Fool!*

A chilly breeze swept over him and raindrops pelted his head and shoulders. He should have made his intentions known to Sarah, but he wasn't ready to propose. Not yet. He didn't want to force Mary to like Sarah. He knew he couldn't, even if he tried. Mary was stubborn. More than likely, she took after him. Even after she helped Mary make jelly and can vegetables, Mary hadn't warmed up to Sarah.

Agonizing over Sarah, Mary and the whole situation had robbed him of sleep for two nights. If he did doze off, images of Sarah in Alvin's arms gave him nightmares.

A gust of wind hurled rain at him, knocking his hat off and spraying water across his face and clothing. Caleb snatched his hat from the ground and took off running toward the porch. Taking the steps two at a time, he reached cover just before sheets of rain poured from the coal-gray sky. A cold tremor shook his body. What if he couldn't take her on another buggy ride or picnic?

The thought nearly stopped his heart. He sat on the porch swing to sort it out, but how could he search his heart when she had taken it with her?

Sarah finished refilling her customers' cups, then started a fresh pot of coffee. During midafternoon, the traffic coming into the bakery slowed, giving her time to tidy up.

The doorbell jangled, but she wanted to finish arranging the baked goods in the display case before she waited on the customer. Straightening up, she braced her hands on her hips. "May I help you?" She froze when she saw it was Caleb.

"I'm sorry I didn't take your news very well," he whispered.

Relief rushed over her. "I should have told you, but we never really had an understanding. I thought it forward to presume we did and try to explain about Alvin."

Caleb glanced over his shoulder, as if something or someone was waiting for him, then back at Sarah. "I have errands to run. I'll come back at five and pick you up. We'll go for a ride, away from stretching ears."

He melted her insides with a smile, giving her gooseflesh on her arms. "*Jah.* I'd like that." Her heart fluttered. "See you later."

She watched him stroll out the door. This time she'd be honest with him.

She closed the shop a few minutes early, ran upstairs and changed into a fresh dress. He arrived right at five o'clock and helped her into the buggy. She fluffed her dress around so it lay in neat folds.

"Giddyap, Snowball." He glanced at her across the seat, his voice deep and rich. "You look lovely, Sarah."

"*Danki.*" Her pulse thudded in time with the horse's clip-clop. He reached over, laid his hand over hers and gave a soft squeeze. A mixture of joy and fear coursed through her veins. What had really changed? Nothing. But it felt like everything had changed.

"Let me speak first." His voice was warm and laced with excitement.

"Okay."

"You're right, we have never had an understanding, but I think you care for me. Is that true?"

"*Jah,*" she said slowly.

"More than just as a friend?"

She hesitated. A smile twitched at the corners of her mouth. *"Jah."*

"Gut. Until we figure out how to get around being from different Orders, can we just have an understanding that we want to see each other?"

Last evening she'd slept fitfully, consumed with the fear of never seeing Caleb and his family again. Now that fear lunged at her throat. She looked out of the buggy and into the one passing on the opposite side of the street. It belonged to Bishop Yoder, and he was staring straight at her.

"Sarah." Caleb snapped her attention back to him.

"Jah. That meets my approval, but as far as the bishop goes, I'm not sure he would agree."

Caleb's desire to have an understanding wasn't exactly what she wanted, but she knew it was the best he could do. She cleared her mind, then gazed out at the field of dark green cornstalks and breathed air with an earthy smell. White and yellow flowers dotted the roadside, and on some stretch of banks, farmers had sown prairie grass that had grown tall and waved invitingly in the breeze.

"We'll stop by and check on the *kinner* before I take you back to town."

Sarah stayed in the kitchen with Mary while Caleb and Jacob went out to do chores. She tilted her head back and inhaled a deep whiff. "Mmm. Something smells *gut*, Mary."

"It's beef stew with vegetables and gravy." Mary pulled some spices out of the oak spice rack and shook them into the boiling concoction.

"That's a lovely spice rack. Did your *daed* make it?"

"*Jah*. On the back, Daed carved, 'You are the spice of my life.' On the oak chest in their bedroom, he carved, 'I'll *liebe* you forever and ever.'"

She stirred the stew and set the spoon on a holder. "He made Mamm the sideboard and the table, too. They have a verse carved on their bottoms, but I can't remember what they say."

A sudden chill ran through Sarah's spine. Apparently Caleb had *liebed* Martha very much. Could he ever *liebe* her as much as he had his late *frau*? Could he set Martha's memory aside or push it into the back of his heart while he let his life go on with another woman?

If she did marry Caleb and moved in here, would she have to share his late *frau*'s house with her? Have constant reminders of Martha everywhere she looked? Would Sarah have to measure up to Martha in his *kinner*'s eyes?

"Sarah," Bishop Yoder called from across the lawn sprawled with congregants after preaching on Church Sunday.

Sarah cringed.

"I'll meet you in the buggy," Hannah said as she retreated far from their paths.

The bishop hurried as best he could with someone either stopping him to talk, greeting him or asking him a question. He wove his way through the throngs of people and breathlessly made it to the tree where Sarah had not budged an inch since he called out her name.

She clenched her fists. *I should have feigned a headache and left after the preaching.*

"We need to set a date for your wedding to Alvin," the bishop blurted.

Sarah straightened her back and sucked in a deep breath. "Bishop, I do not want to marry Alvin. I don't like him."

The bishop stared at her with cold, steely eyes. "You haven't tried. Go for a buggy ride with him so you can get to know him."

She stood with her lips pressed tightly for a long while. Then she found the courage to speak. "*Nein.* Caleb Brenneman and I have an understanding."

"What did you say?" His voice rose with an edge to it.

"At the appropriate time, we will make a commitment to one another." After she said it aloud, it sounded strange even to her. Exactly what did that mean? He never really used the word *marry*.

At the time, his words had sounded like a commitment. But now she wasn't so sure.

He laughed. "Is that what he said to you?"

She nodded. Moisture started trickling down her forehead and onto her brows.

"He did not tell you he would change to our more orthodox affiliation, did he?"

"Well, we haven't really discussed it."

"Nein, I imagine he hasn't. You need to discuss it, Sarah. Remember, you can't leave the church. He must rejoin the Old Order. What is he waiting for? I'll tell you what—for you to get used to his ways and their softer lifestyle. Ask him, Sarah. You'll see."

She glared at the bishop. She had fallen for Caleb and hoped he felt the same about her. Enough so he would change to the Old Order. *Nein*, Caleb had never mentioned it. She'd been lying to herself thinking it wouldn't make a difference to Caleb. That he would eventually offer to change. Only he hadn't, at least not yet.

"Sarah." The bishop jarred her out of her thoughts. Glaring at her, he said, "You must choose. But remember, giving up your church means shunning."

Jah, she had much to think about.

Sarah puttered around the apartment, watering plants and trying to decide how to approach the subject again with Caleb. A few weeks ago, every day seemed the same, but life was simpler. She had the bakery, and helped with church events and community projects. Now her life felt like it was being tossed around like a ball hanging on a string from a paddle.

The garden was always the place where she did her best thinking. Sarah unhooked her gardening smock and pinned it to cover her dress. After grabbing her tools from the closet, she headed downstairs and out back to till the garden. Sarah lowered her knees to a mat, pressed the blade of the hoe between each row and uprooted every annoying thistle and weed.

She worked until almost dark, clearing the path and loosening the soil between the rows of carrots, cabbage and lettuce. She took a sniff of the fragrant parsley and cilantro. "With a *gut* clean bed around you, you will flourish."

She weeded and watered the tomato plants. They would soon have red fruit. She was glad now she'd started them in the winter.

The hard physical movements drained her energy, and she still hadn't come to a decision. The bishop's words haunted her. As hard as she tried to forget them, they fought their way back to the forefront. She hated to admit it, but the bishop was right. Caleb knew the problem. He had to join her church, not the other way around. *Jah*, he took her to Bible study and to meet his Sunday school class so she would get to know them, like them and want to join them.

If the bishop had found out that she'd attended a function with the New Order community, he would have disciplined her. And rightly so. Caleb wanted to sway her to his side...his church.

She hadn't realized it before. It was as plain as a sign tacked on a tree.

Chapter Eleven

Sarah stayed busy the next three weeks, testing recipes for her cookbook and neglecting her garden. She made room in the display case for the three batches of new cookie recipes she'd developed—spiced apple, spiced oatmeal raisin and vegan carrot—and then added the announcement to the chalkboard. She cut up several cookies of each kind and laid the small pieces on a plate and set the plate at the front of the counter.

Throughout the day, she received compliments on her new recipes. At the end of the day, she cleaned the display case and realized the new cookies had sold out. *Ach.* They liked them!

Sarah pulled out the empty trays, carried them back to the kitchen and waved them in front of Hannah. "What do you think of this?"

"Congratulations. Now, how about creating a new cake recipe or two?"

"I've been toying with a couple of ideas."

Sarah carted out the ingredients for a new pistachio-crunch cake. She stirred them all together and popped the two layers in the oven. Grabbing a pen, she made updates on the recipe card until the bishop's words forced their way into her head again. She hated to admit it, but he was right. Either Caleb or she had to give up their church.

If neither of them wanted to change to the other person's church, they needed to end their relationship. The trouble was, she had grown very fond of Jacob…and Caleb.

Sarah pulled the cake pans out of the oven and set them to cool. She finished cleaning the bakery, and just as she reached out to flip the sign on the front door to Closed, a nose poked against the glass door. She jumped back and laughed. The door pushed open and she wrapped Jacob in a hug.

She straightened her posture and smoothed her skirt. Her attention darted to Caleb. "It's closing time. I'm out of coffee and rolls."

"That's okay, we didn't come to eat." Caleb motioned to his *sohn* to speak.

Jacob looked down and scuffed the toe of his shoe on the floor like he was kicking a rock. "Sarah, I never get to see you. Can I come and work in the bakery?" His voice wavered.

Her heart melted. "I miss you, too, Jacob."

When he faced her, loneliness dampened his eyes, but she had the perfect way to dry them. "Your garden is spotless and mine is in desperate need of care. How would you like to help me weed and prune bushes?"

Jacob let out a silly laugh. "I will have your garden spick-and-span in no time at all."

"How about Monday afternoon?"

Jacob looked at his *daed*. Caleb nodded. "We'll come by after lunch."

On Monday, Jacob hoed between the rows of vegetables, weeded around the tomatoes, and then grabbed the hose and watered the garden. When he finished, he weeded her flowers in the corner of the yard, carried buckets of water and thoroughly drenched each plant.

Caleb had brought his work gloves. As fast as Sarah could trim the bushes, he gathered the bush clippings and weeds from Jacob's work into a nice pile. She drew a quick breath at the touch of his hand cupping her elbow. "Let me do that for a while. Your arms and shoulders must be getting tired."

Sarah heaved a sigh. "I suppose so. The yard work has gone unattended far too long. Thank you and Jacob for all your help."

He nodded. "My pleasure."

"Mine, too, Daed. I'm a big help."

"Indeed you are," Sarah assured Jacob.

Tears threatened to fall at their sweet words, but Sarah choked them back. "It is very nice of you both to help me." She waited for Caleb to speak and say something like "you need an *ehemann*," but he didn't. It would definitely be a lot easier if she did have an *ehemann*. But one of her choice. Not chosen for her by the bishop.

Sarah propped her hands on her hips. "I just have one question. If we work hard together, we should also have fun together. What should we do? Go fishing and take a picnic lunch?"

Jacob's eyes grew big. "*Jah*. Let's do that." His gaze drifted to his *daed*. Caleb slowly let a smile play at the corners of his mouth. "Let's have our outing on Sunday afternoon."

Sarah brightened. It would be nice having the whole afternoon with Caleb and his family. And maybe it would give her an opportunity to talk to Caleb alone and ask him if he would change to Old Order.

She locked the door behind them. A giddy sensation welled deep in her heart. She didn't know how she and Caleb would solve their faith difference, but it just had to work out.

Before the bishop declared her shunned.

Sunday was here in no time. Mary had made plans with friends, but Jacob was up just after dawn. Caleb flooded a patch of ground with water and Jacob sat waiting. Caleb finished the chores and gathered their fishing poles and bucket then wandered over to Jacob, where he was digging up worms. "I can almost taste those fresh fish right now."

Jacob smacked his lips. "Me, too. Can Sarah stay for supper?"

Caleb's feet stuttered to a stop. "I don't know, Jacob. It might be too late by the time we get back." Caleb's stomach twisted into a knot. He couldn't tell his *sohn* that Sarah's bishop wouldn't allow that type of behavior from a single woman.

"Maybe another day." Jacob grabbed the bucket of worms and carried it to the buggy.

Caleb stowed their fishing poles on the floor of the buggy. "We should hurry. Sarah will be expecting us."

Sarah was ready to go with a picnic basket all packed when they pulled up in their buggy. Jacob held a bowl of cookies while Sarah climbed in and settled on the seat. "Guess what, Sarah?" Without waiting, he rushed on. "Daed and I dug worms this morning, and they are ready to go to work."

"*Gut.* I'm hoping you will show me how to fish. It has been a long time since I last held a pole and cast a hook in the water."

Jacob puffed his chest. "I'll put the worm on your hook and show you how to cast. It's easy."

Caleb nodded. "Jacob is an experienced fisherman. The last time we visited the English River, he caught two bluegills and one catfish to my one bluegill."

Jacob removed his hat and twirled it around in his hand like Caleb often did. "I'm the bestest, huh, Daed?"

"Indeed you are." Caleb parked the buggy under a tree along the bank of the river. While Sarah spread out the lunch, Caleb and Jacob found just the right spot to throw their lines in the water. They laid out their poles, tackle box and stringer.

Sarah laid a blanket on the ground and sat the picnic basket on one corner to hold it down when the breeze kicked up. She set the sandwiches, chips and salad in the center with the paper products. "Why don't you guys have a bite to eat before we start fishing?"

Caleb smiled as Jacob hurried to the blanket to sit next to Sarah. That left Caleb sitting on the opposite side, with the food in between them. But the more he brought Jacob to see Sarah, the more attached Jacob became to her. Which meant he needed to approach the subject of Sarah changing to New Order and soon. Of course that would mean he'd have to ask her to marry him. Was he truly prepared to do that?

Jacob chattered away. "Sarah, if you catch a catfish, you have to be very careful because their fins are sharp. But don't worry, I'll help you."

"*Danki.* I would really appreciate that."

"We didn't bring any minnows, only worms and bobbers." Jacob finished his last bite of sandwich. "I'll put the worm on the hook for you because it has to be done right or he can slip off and get away."

"My, you are very knowledgeable. I'm glad you are here to help me."

"Daed, can we fish now?"

Sarah gestured to the river. "Go ahead while I pack up the rest of our lunch, then I'll be right there."

Caleb opened the bucket of worms, and he and Jacob put the wiggly things on their hooks. Jacob walked down the bank and stepped on a rock by the river, then stepped farther out onto another rock. "Be careful, Jacob. The rocks will be slick."

"*Jah*, I am." Jacob's feet wobbled. His hook and line swung back and forth.

"Jacob, watch the hook," Caleb yelled as he threw down his pole and ran toward the *bu*.

Jacob reached up, grabbed the swinging hook and line, and caught the hook deep in his finger. "Ouch!"

Caleb grabbed Jacob and whirled him around to the grassy bank as Sarah ran down the slope. "Hold the pole, Sarah, while I grab the tackle box."

She dropped to her knees, put one arm around Jacob's shoulders and held the pole with the other. Caleb cut the fishing line, threw the pole on the ground and carried Jacob up the bank. "Sarah, sit and hold Jacob while I take out the hook."

"*Nein*, Daed." Jacob screamed. "It hurts too much."

Sarah's stomach turned a somersault as she sensed Jacob's pain from the tensing of his body. She held Jacob protectively and tossed Caleb a warning look.

Caleb's voice turned soothing. "Jacob, calm down and listen to me. The hook is all the way in past the barb, so I cannot pull it out the same way it went in. I need to cut off both ends, then push it through your finger. It is a small hook, so it will only go in a little ways. We have talked about this before. Will you be a big *bu* and let me work? It will only take a minute, and Sarah will help you hold your hand very still."

Jacob sniffled and tears rolled down his cheek. "Okay, but hurry."

He patted Jacob on the shoulder. "I will." He looked at Sarah. "Steady his hand."

Caleb cleaned the area with antiseptic and dried the finger. He pushed the hook through the pad of Jacob's finger, guiding it out the side while Jacob only let out a whimper. He cut off the barb and eye, then pulled the shank out with the pliers. Jacob moaned but did not move or cry. Caleb held gauze on Jacob's finger until the bleeding stopped, then cleaned the area and bandaged the fingertip.

When Caleb finished, Jacob leaned back against Sarah and sobbed.

"Jacob, you are a big *bu*." Caleb's voice was soft, yet firm.

"Caleb, I'll take care of Jacob while you pack up the buggy."

Sarah hugged Jacob close and whispered in his ear. "If you need to cry to release the pain, then you cry. That's why *Gott* gave us tears." She rubbed his back with the palm of her hand until exhaustion tackled his body and pulled him into a restless sleep. Tears filled her eyes and emotion clogged her throat. She was proud of this little man for holding perfectly still as Caleb had pushed the hook through his finger. Not many grown men would have been able to stay perfectly still and not let out a yelp. But this small *bu* proved to be as strong-willed as a man.

She blotted her tears and held this sweet little soul, wishing he were hers. It was harder each time she saw Jacob to let him go home without her. Yet she had no choice. She had planned to bring up the subject of their churches with Caleb, but now was not the time. But how could she let this frail *bu* go home? Would Mary comfort him?

Jacob tossed his head back and sobbed. "I want my *mamm*. Are you my *mamm*?"

Sarah jerked her head up and looked at Caleb as he approached. His startled eyes locked with hers. She patted Jacob's head and held it close to her. "Jacob, I am so sorry this happened. I will drive out tomorrow just to see you and spend the whole afternoon taking care of you."

Jacob's sobs quieted and his shoulders slumped in total surrender, trusting her to his care. Apparently he accepted her words as a motherly gesture.

Caleb lifted Jacob off Sarah's lap and set him in the buggy while Sarah gathered her picnic basket. After she climbed in, he stowed the basket on the floor by the seat. He tapped the reins on Snowball's back, and the horse set to work with a jerk of the buggy. "I'll take Sarah home to the bakery, Jacob. Then I'll get you home."

"*Nein.* Sarah wants to come home with me. Don't you?"

Sarah hesitated. "Is Mary home?"

Caleb shrugged. "She should be, but she might still be with her friends."

"Let's take Jacob to your house. I can tuck him into bed and sit with him for a while before you take me home."

Caleb glanced at Jacob and nodded.

The few miles to Caleb's farm seemed like an eternity. While Caleb helped Jacob into bed, Sarah heated a glass of milk for him. She tiptoed into the room and sat in the chair that Caleb had pulled next to the bed. "I'll stay with him for a while, but Mary has returned home."

"*Gut.* I'll do chores, then take you home."

She nodded but kept her gaze firmly on Jacob. When Caleb left the room, she leaned back in the chair, her pulse pounding with fear. It nearly tore a hole in her heart to see Jacob in pain.

How could she ever leave this little *bu*?

On Monday Sarah left the bakery early after instructing Hannah to close. She hitched King, treated him to a slice of apple and patted his nose. "Your legs will get a *gut* stretching today."

Caleb hurried out of the *haus* when she arrived. "Jacob's been wondering when you'd get here."

"How is he?"

"I think better than he wants to let on, but his finger looks swollen."

"*Ach.* I'll take care of that right away. His finger is probably throbbing."

Caleb held the door for Sarah as she dashed

through. Mary stood at the sink and turned as she entered. "*Hullo*, Mary."

"*Hullo.*"

Sarah sprinted up the stairs and tapped lightly on Jacob's door.

"Come in," his tiny voice whispered from the other side.

She darted in, felt Jacob's forehead and examined the finger. "No fever, but I'll wrap some ice in a cloth and get that swelling down."

He jerked his hand back. "Will that hurt?"

"*Nein.* It will feel much better when the swelling is gone." She hurried to get the ice and returned in minutes. She propped his hand and gently applied the cold compress.

Jacob's eyes looked weary but he smiled. "I like it when you take care of me, Sarah. When I'm better, I'll help you with your garden."

Sarah grinned. *Jah*, the more time she spent with Jacob, the more she didn't ever want to leave his side. If the bishop found out about her two trips out here when he'd strictly forbidden it, she would surely be disciplined.

Chapter Twelve

The bell on the bakery door rang loudly in late afternoon as Jacob burst through, ran straight to Sarah and gave her a big hug. "*Danki* for coming to visit me when I hurt my finger."

"I was glad to do it. Since this is your first visit since the accident, you may pick out a special treat on me."

While Jacob searched the display case, Caleb stepped forward. "Mary's birthday is Sunday, and I was wondering if you'd make her a cake. Strawberry is her favorite. We'll have a small gathering for her in the afternoon at about four o'clock. Hannah's also invited."

"Sure, I'd be happy to do that for Mary."

"*Danki.* She won't be expecting it. Did you hear that, Jacob? It's a surprise."

"*Jah.* I won't tell."

Caleb pointed to a roll. Sarah pulled the cinnamon swirl out of the case, placed it on a plate and poured his coffee. By then Jacob had selected a Bismarck with powdered sugar on top.

When Sarah had a minute, she stole away from the counter and sat next to Jacob. He held up his finger. "See my scar?" A little sadness edged his words.

"Oh my, that is a handsome scar, and you have a great story to tell about getting it."

Jacob looked at his finger with a proud glint in his eye.

"And it is *gut* to see that it has not hurt your appetite," she said as she glanced at his clean plate. "Caleb, King needs to have his legs stretched. Maybe I could drive out after I close and pick a few strawberries."

"After Jacob and I run a few errands, we will start home. You can pick as many as you want."

After locking up and hitching King, Sarah headed the buggy down the road toward Caleb's farm. The summer breeze twirled the strings of her prayer *kapp* and rustled the leaves on the cornstalks. The musical sound of King's hooves clip-clopping on the road, the birds singing and the bees buzzing by made the three-mile trip seem short.

The soaking rain from the day before still blanketed the ground, giving off an earthy smell. How she loved the country. She hadn't traveled outside of the Midwest and didn't want to. She couldn't imagine leaving all this behind.

When she met a farmer on a tractor pulling a wagon, she tugged the reins, maneuvering King to the far side of the road in case the vehicle's noise disturbed the horse. But it didn't. King was a well-disciplined horse.

Sarah guided the buggy into Caleb's barnyard, stopped and looked around as she stepped from her buggy. Caleb's farm was quiet. She didn't see Caleb or Jacob. Not even Tiger and her kittens were around to greet her.

She walked through the strawberry patch, hoping to find at least a few plump red fruits for Mary's cake. *Jah*. She pulled one from the plant and popped it in her mouth. *Mmm*. They would taste *wunderbaar* in Mary's birthday cake.

Ach. She'd forgotten a container for the strawberries. Mary wouldn't mind if she borrowed one. She strolled to the back porch and knocked on the door.

No answer.

She knocked again and listened for footfalls.

The breeze rustled a nearby field of grain, birds chirped and grasshoppers jumped through the grass, but silence creeped from the *haus*.

She turned the doorknob and the door swung open. "Mary. Are you home?"

Sarah stepped into the kitchen, listened, but the only sound was the ticking of a clock.

Poking her nose in the cupboards first, she looked around for a container. Only dishes sat on the shelves. She opened the pantry door and found a small empty box that was the right size stacked on top of other containers. She'd return it before Mary even noticed it was missing.

The tidiness of the *haus* caught her attention. She surrendered to curiosity and entered the living room. How did a thirteen-year-old girl manage to keep the house so clean and neat with all the other household chores?

Sarah understood how Mary missed her *mamm*. She missed hers, as well. A young woman needed a *mamm* to fuss over her, to help her prepare when she got married and to be there when she had her first *boppli*.

She strolled around the living room, looking at Martha's quilt rack, her mending and her basket of scrap material from quilting. Suddenly an idea popped into her head for a gift to give Mary for her birthday that would remind her every day of her *mamm*.

On Sunday, after preaching and the noon meal were finished, Sarah climbed into her buggy and flopped on the seat. "I had no idea that Alvin Studer and Bertha Bontrager were getting married until the banns were read today. No wonder I haven't seen the bishop or Alvin lately."

Hannah settled on the seat next to her. "You don't sound happy. I would think you would be shouting for joy." Hannah's voice rose in puzzlement.

Sarah didn't want to marry Alvin, but somehow the loss of him hit her hard. She was now envious of him, of what he had. She was happy for them, and imagined Alvin was getting ready right now, as was the custom, to ride around, inviting his family to the wedding.

"Don't be silly, Hannah." But loneliness drained Sarah's heart until it seemed as hollow as an old dead log. "I'll stop by the bakery and we can pick up the cake and mints and head out to Caleb's farm."

Sarah trotted King at an easy pace. Hannah held Mary's birthday cake on her knees and the mints she'd made sat on the seat between them.

"Don't hit a bump. I don't want to spoil your cake." Hannah shot her a warning look.

"You must be planning on a big piece. Strawberry is one of your favorites, too." Sarah tossed her a smile.

"Not this time. I decided if I were ever going to catch an *ehemann*, I'd have to lose some weight. I started my diet and have lost ten pounds so far."

"Hannah, I'm so proud of you."

Hannah smiled proudly as they pulled onto Caleb's farm.

Caleb watched the buggy approach, waited and helped them down, then escorted them into the house. "Mary, look who's here."

Caleb introduced Sarah and Hannah to his *bruder*, Peter, and his *frau*, Lillia. They greeted each other.

Mary's eyes glowed when Sarah uncovered the cake. A two-layer cake covered in frosting with strawberries and whipped cream on top.

"It's a *wunderbaar* cake and looks delicious," Mary gasped. *"Danki."*

Lillia agreed. "Looks *gut*."

Caleb smiled at Sarah and gave her a wink. "Let's set the table, and I'll get the ice cream. Sit, Mary. It's your birthday. We'll handle this."

"I want a big piece." Jacob scooted out a chair and plunked himself down.

"Of course, and I hope you try one of my mints, too." Hannah held the plate out to Jacob, smiled and nodded toward the mints.

He took a red one. "Mmm. That tastes like strawberries."

When they finished eating, Sarah pulled Mary's gift out of her bag. "Mary, this is for you. I took some of the scraps left over from your *mamm*'s leaf quilts and made a Bible cover and sewed one of her leaves on top."

Mary gasped and her face turned red. "You had no right! You took them without permission! How could you? I had plans for those scraps." She raked the legs of her chair back over the flooring as she stood, then ran out of the house, letting the screen door bang behind her.

"Daed, tell Mary she can't slam the door."

"Mind your business, Jacob. It's not your job to worry about Mary's actions."

"Jacob, I've heard a lot about Tiger and her kittens. Could I see them?" Hannah popped a mint in her mouth and stood.

He nodded, jumped off the chair and headed for the door. "You're going to *liebe* them. If you want one, I'll give it to you."

"Jacob," Caleb said stiffly.

"Okay. You don't *have* to take one." Hannah followed Jacob out the door.

"We must be going, *bruder.* Tell the *kinner* we had to leave." Peter patted Caleb on the back. "It was nice to meet you, Sarah."

Lillia gave Sarah a smile. "Don't worry, Sarah. Mary will get over it."

When the door closed, Sarah turned toward Caleb. "I'm so sorry, Caleb. They were scraps. I'd *nein* idea how badly it would hurt Mary. I thought she would like it."

"I'll talk to Mary. It was a shock. If you hadn't told her where they came from, it would have been a year before she noticed. She was very close to her *mamm,* and it hit a sensitive spot." He glanced at the door Mary had slammed. A line of worry etched across his forehead.

"I hope she doesn't think I was trying to steal the position that her *mamm* holds in her heart. That wasn't my intention."

"She'll get over it." Caleb's soothing voice wrapped around her like a hug.

Sarah stepped back. Her mouth was like a desert and all her words had dried up. She'd messed up badly.

Mary would never forgive her.

The next day, Sarah coaxed King into a faster trot as the buggy neared Caleb's farm. Drizzle changed to light rain when she turned into his drive. The wind kicked up, blowing dirt out of the fields and filling the air with a wet, muddy smell. The sky darkened with black clouds tumbling and rolling overhead. She tugged on the reins. "Whoa, King."

Caleb ran from the house and helped her down. "Go on in, and I'll put King in the barn."

She hurried up the steps and waited on the porch. She removed her cape and shook off the moisture, wishing it were that easy to shake away the mistake she'd made by taking Martha's scraps of material.

Caleb jumped the porch steps two at a time. "What brings you out here on a messy day like this?"

"I couldn't sleep a wink last night. I'm still fretting over how I hurt Mary. I saw the basket of scraps and thought she'd like the cover if it reminded her of her *mamm*. My heart is still aching over that stupid mistake."

"Don't beat yourself up, Sarah. She needs a little time to think about it. Mary would rather cook and clean than sew. I think she left the scraps sitting in the living room because they reminded her of her *mamm*, and she didn't know what else to do with them. You did nothing wrong. Someday, Mary will treasure what you did for her, but maybe not today." He shrugged.

"We talked a little when we canned, and it sounded like she was getting through grieving her *mamm*. I thought it'd be okay, but I should have asked. Can I talk to her?"

"She's in the kitchen." Caleb smiled and held the door open.

Sarah walked in slowly, as though she were a child going to the teacher for a scolding. She crossed the large room and stood by the table, propping her hip against it for support. Mary remained at the stove, cooking something that smelled like chicken and dumplings. If she heard her enter, she never acknowledged Sarah's presence.

"*Hullo*, Mary. I wanted to tell you again how sorry I am. If you want, I can pull the stitching from the cover and put the scraps back."

"That's not necessary. I thought maybe one day I'd think of something to do with them, but it's a nice cover." Mary remained facing the stove.

"When you're ready to can vegetables again, I'll be more than happy to help."

"*Danki* for the offer." Mary kept her back toward Sarah.

One thing was for sure and for certain.

Mary would never forgive her.

Chapter Thirteen

After the next preaching, Sarah hurried to disappear from Bishop Yoder's sight. She kept a brisk pace, turned the corner and headed for the door.

"Sarah." His footsteps thumped closer with each stride.

The thought of surrender had never occurred to her before, but his persistence had worn her down. She frowned, then stopped and turned around. "Bishop, did you call my name?"

"*Jah*. And after I did, it looked like your step had a livelier spring to it toward the door."

"Sorry. Thoughts preoccupied my mind. What did you need to see me about?"

"Do you know Ezra Smith?"

Exasperation sent a chill charging through her, but she shook it off. "I've seen him, but I don't really know him."

"He is a widower with two small *kinner*, and

he'd like to meet you. How about tomorrow?" His rigid stance spoke volumes.

"*Nein*, Monday is not good. Tuesday is better." She started easing toward the door.

"He'll stop by the bakery, and perhaps he'll ask you on a buggy ride."

Sarah glanced over the bishop's right shoulder and noticed others gawking and seemingly edging in their direction. "I'll bake something special and look forward to meeting him."

The bishop's mouth practically hit the floor in surprise. Then he cleared his throat. "Have an enjoyable day."

"You, too, Bishop." She headed to her buggy, where Hannah waited, wearing a smile.

"What was that all about?"

"I think the bishop and I might have come to some kind of an understanding, although he doesn't know it yet."

Hannah raised a brow. "What does that mean?"

"You'll see soon enough."

Sarah guided her buggy up Caleb's driveway. The crunching of gravel under the wheels appeared to snag Caleb's attention from watering his garden. He dropped the hose and hurried to meet her.

"*Gut* mornin'. You're here early." His smile warmed her heart.

"*Jah*. Is Mary ready to can tomatoes?"

"They are already in a hot-water bath." He gave King a pat.

"*Ach*. I'm late. Canning is an all-day ordeal, so I'd better get to it." She handed him the sack of bread and cookies she had brought, latched on to his offered arm and stepped to the ground. "There's a basket with potato salad and fried chicken on the floor of the buggy. Please bring it in."

"*Danki* for helping Mary." His words tangled in the sounds of her grabbing the sack and running for the house.

Sweltering heat hit Sarah in the face as she entered the kitchen, and the smell of cooking tomatoes permeated the air. She sat her sack on the table and then stood next to Mary at the stove. Plumes of steam rose from the kettles of simmering fruit. The breeze streaming through the open window did little to cool the room.

Caleb set the basket in the propane-powered refrigerator and tossed Sarah a smile on his way out the door.

"Mornin', Mary. I'm ready to work."

"Mornin'. Sure you want to? It's really hot in here." Mary grabbed the towel slung over her shoulder and wiped the dripping perspiration from her face.

"*Jah*." Sarah pushed up her sleeves, grabbed a

spoon and started packing the mason jars Mary had already washed and sterilized.

She'd worked nearly an hour, and Mary hadn't said two words to her except what the work required. Guilt inched up Sarah's spine. It was crystal clear. Mary would never forgive her for taking the fabric scraps and making the book cover.

Beads of sweat rolled down Sarah's back. She walked to the window and stood in front of the breeze for several minutes.

Mary looked at her and smiled. "Hot?"

"Jah."

"Me, too."

At four o'clock, the jars filled, Sarah helped Mary clean the kitchen. "I'm exhausted." She tidied her dress, wiped off splatters, and washed her face and hands. "Let me know when more tomatoes are ready to can."

"Danki for your help." Mary's no-nonsense attitude made it plain she'd tolerate her presence, but she'd no longer confide in her.

Sarah pulled her potato salad and chicken out of the refrigerator and placed them on the table next to Mary's marinated, sliced red tomatoes and a loaf of bread. While she set the plates and silverware on the table, Mary rang the dinner bell.

Judging from the silence at the table and the small amount of food on the plates, it was too uncomfortable to eat in a sweltering-hot kitchen.

Jacob picked at his chicken and barely touched his potato salad. "Jacob, do you like the dinner?"

"I'm too hot to eat. Since you canned tomatoes with Mary, can you help me with the garden?" Jacob puffed out his lower lip. "You never help me."

"Jacob." Caleb's firm tone held a warning.

Jacob kicked the chair. "It's not fair! She never comes to help me anymore!" He jumped off the chair and ran out the kitchen's screen door, letting it bang twice before it shut.

"Jacob, get back here," Caleb bellowed. Jacob sidled up to the door. "Apologize to Sarah right now."

His chin almost touched his chest, but his brooding gray eyes peered up. "I'm sorry, Sarah." He ran down the porch steps and headed across the lawn.

Sarah followed him out the door. Jacob was right. She'd spent a lot of time with Mary, but she couldn't spend much more time at Caleb's farm or someone would find out and tell the bishop. "Jacob, wait."

"That's okay." But his shaky voice told her it wasn't.

Caleb laid a warm and soothing hand on her shoulder. "He'll get over it. We'll think of some way you can spend time with him." He winked. "I'll hitch King up for you."

Sarah blew out a heavy breath. "Tell Jacob I'll help him next time."

As he tightened the girth around King, a worry hovered in the back of his mind. Eventually the bishop would hear of her visits to his farm. *Nein*, they had to think of other ways to spend time together, and Sarah would have to quit helping Mary.

Caleb waited in the driveway with the buggy.

Her steps were slow but sure to where he waited. He took her basket and set it on the seat. "You look tired."

"*Jah*. The heat and the canning sapped my energy." A moment of silence settled between them as they watched a few robins scamper around, looking for their supper.

"I'll stop by one day this week." He backed away from the buggy.

"That'll be nice." The breeze picked up and snapped the tie strings to her prayer *kapp*. "Sure, now the wind blows, when we're *done* canning."

Caleb laughed. "Sounds like you think the breeze schemed against you and Mary while you canned."

She chuckled. "I didn't mean it quite like that." Sarah stepped into the buggy. "Caleb, I have something I need to tell you. Because of the incident with Alvin, I need to explain so there's no misunderstanding." Sarah let her gaze fall on his shirt. She lifted her chin and her eyes clouded with a mist.

"What's up?" Uneasiness tugged at his nerves. Was something said when he left the kitchen?

"The bishop donned his matchmaking hat again. He wants me to spend time with Ezra Smith. He is a widower with two *kinner*. I have no desire to marry him, but I wanted to show the bishop that I believe in supporting my community."

The smile slid from his face. His heart dropped to his feet. He froze. He stared at her. Gott, *You took away Martha and now You're taking away Sarah.*

"I must trust *Gott* to guide my heart and my head, but know that this is only to appease the bishop."

He fought to find his voice. "*Jah*, I understand." His voice cracked. "It's hard when your religion is based on community. You must decide what is right for you, but I will miss your company."

"Please let me know when Mary is ready to do more canning. She's still young and should have help with such things."

"*Danki* for your thoughtfulness, Sarah."

He held out his hand to her. She grasped it and squeezed. When he took it away, it was as if a cool breeze had swept over his heart. He would miss her warm touch.

Caleb watched as Sarah's buggy drove away, kicking up dust that swirled around and drifted away. His chest ached as if she'd torn his heart out, wadded it up and tossed it into that dust cloud. He gulped a deep breath of air. The strength drained from his body. He tried to take a step, but couldn't. Not yet. Not until she was out of sight. It was silly the way his insides did somersaults whenever she was near and felt like a hollowed-out log when she left.

Jah, he needed to get a moment alone with Sarah and ask her if she would change to the New Order. Then he'd know what to do next.

The first of July, but he felt like it was January in Iowa and it was twenty below zero.

Sarah rose early to get a head start on baking. She paused for a moment to review Thursday's list. Yesterday, for the first time, the bakery had sold out of baked goods. She mixed up the yeast rolls, increased the recipe to make three dozen more, covered the bowl and set it aside.

Footfalls across the bakery shop's floor soon found their way to the kitchen. Hannah plopped her hip against the table. "I was practically up all night, helping Mamm and Daed pack for their trip to Missouri. Thanks for starting the baking on your own. I'll work hard to make up for being late."

"Gut." Sarah pointed at the list. "You can bake the cookies. I promised the bishop to make something special for Ezra's visit." Hannah nodded and headed to her work area.

Sarah mentally reviewed the recipes while she loaded her arms with the ingredients to make apple fritters and an apple strudel. Men had a hard time resisting fritters and strudel. She dumped it all on her workspace, then fetched the ten-pound bag of apples and set it on the sink.

While Hannah started the cookies, Sarah peeled, cored and diced apples. She stirred up the strudel, added part of the apples and popped it in the oven. She made the fritter batter with the remaining apples. After grabbing a pan from the rack, she heated the oil and dropped the fritters in until they were golden brown. After they cooled, she drizzled a glaze over top.

Midmorning, the bakery door opened and Ezra Smith timidly entered and gave her a shy nod. He wandered casually in front of the display case as if trying to make a decision, and every so often glanced her way.

She smiled at his attempt to make this visit look casual. *"Gut* mornin', Ezra. *Welkum."*

Hannah peeked around the doorway but disappeared back into the kitchen.

"It all looks *gut*, but I will take an apple fritter and a cup of coffee." He paused. "And two of the chocolate-frosted cake donuts to take home."

Sarah handed him the sack of donuts. She placed a fritter on a plate and a sugar cookie on another, poured two cups of coffee, and set it all on a tray. She led the way to a table and set her coffee and cookie across from him. "I'll keep you company, if you don't mind."

Ezra pulled out a chair for her and one for him. He slid his hat on the empty seat nearby.

Sarah sipped her coffee and settled back in the chair. Ezra had a handsome face with a wide jaw, but it gave him character. His sandy-colored hair looked *gut* with his sun-bronzed face.

"This is a delicious fritter, Sarah. Did you make it?"

"Jah. Danki." She folded her hands in her lap.

He nodded to her plate. *"Datt's* a cute sugar cookie in the shape of a dog." Ezra's eyes sparkled and little crinkles etched around them when he laughed.

"Hannah likes them. She's my assistant. It reminds her of her dog, Mint-Candy."

He chuckled. *"Datt's* a funny name for a dog."

"When you see Hannah, ask her how he got his name."

"My *kinner* are home with my sister." He

pointed to a sugar cookie. "They would like your bakery very much."

"*Jah*. Most *kinner* do."

He propped an elbow on the table and leaned closer to her. "My large farm keeps me busy growing vegetables to sell at the canneries and at auction. I also raise hogs and cattle. If I have more *sohns*, I could buy more land and expand my produce. Then the farm would be large enough to support more than one family."

Ezra smiled shyly. "I hope to find a woman who shares my interests."

The heat burned on her cheeks. She glanced down at the table instead of into his deep brown eyes.

"Ah, Sarah, don't blush. We are friends, talking. *Jah?*" His voice was smooth as whipped cream.

Ezra had shared his hopes and dreams already, unlike Caleb, who often drove her the three miles from his farm to town and hardly said two words to her. She already knew what Ezra wanted but hadn't yet discovered what Caleb saw for his future.

In all fairness, though, Caleb was a typical farmer, who drove slowly, gawking at his neighbors' fields and comparing them to his own. He measured his farm's growing progress during the season against other farms around his. Ezra might do the same, but he also communicated well.

"Sarah?"

"Sorry. I was thinking about how much work you do. *Danki* for stopping in today."

He smiled. "Even a farmer has to take time off. That gives me an idea. Tomorrow, I'm taking my *kinner* to the Washington County Fair. I'd like for you to join us."

She'd never been to a fair before. Daed would grumble he was too busy for that kind of nonsense. She'd known others who visited the fair and raved about all the fun they had. "I'd like that very much, Ezra." Then a twinge of regret pierced her, but it was too late to take her answer back.

"See you at nine tomorrow morning, and wear comfortable shoes." He grabbed his hat from the chair and flashed a broad smile before he nodded goodbye and walked out the bakery door.

Chapter Fourteen

Friday dawned with a cloudless blue sky, giving Sarah the inspiration to pack a light lunch for a picnic at the fair. At five minutes to nine o'clock, she carried her bag out to the porch and sat on the step to wait. The rented vehicle and driver arrived on time. Ezra opened the back door, and she slid in next to a couple of sandy-haired cuties who were the spitting image of their *daed*.

Ezra hopped back in the front of the SUV next to the driver, turned around and looked at his *kinner*. "This is Beth and David." He tilted his head toward Sarah. "This is Sarah Gingerich."

She smiled. "Nice to meet you both."

"Miss Sarah, are you excited about going to the fair?" Beth's amber eyes sparkled as she spoke.

"Very much so. I've never attended the fair before." She pressed a hand to her stomach to stop the fluttering of a giant butterfly.

"Really?" Ezra said. "Your folks never took you?"

"*Nein*. They were always too busy in the bakery."

"You'll have a *gut* time. I'm glad I'm the one who gets to show it to you," Ezra said.

Sarah swallowed a sigh. Was he getting interested in her already? Had she misled him?

Ezra talked to her for a while, then started talking to the driver about farming. The *kinner* acted as if they had forgotten she was there and started discussing what they wanted to do and see first at the fair. She relaxed in her seat and enjoyed the scenery for the twenty-minute drive to the fairgrounds.

They stepped out of the SUV, and Ezra arranged a time for the driver to pick them up. He swung his arm with a sweeping movement toward the midway. "Sarah, the fun awaits you." Ezra stayed close beside her as the *kinner* walked ahead. After a short distance, the *kinner* stopped to look at a game of chance, but Ezra motioned them along.

When they came to the cotton candy vendor, David gave Ezra a puppy-dog look. "*Daed*, please, can we have some?"

Ezra paid and the man handed David and Beth each a stick of what looked like swirls of spun cotton wrapped around it. He held a stick out to

Sarah. She shook her head. "I've never eaten it before. I don't know if I'd like it."

Ezra took the stick. "You've never had cotton candy? Now's your chance. We'll share." He grabbed a hunk, and pulled it off. "See, like this," he said, and stuffed it in his mouth. "Your turn."

She pulled off a small, sticky amount and stuck it in her mouth. "Oh. It's delicious and practically melts in your mouth." She smiled. "That was fun to eat. What is it?"

"Spun sugar." Ezra's tongue had a tinge of blue coloring. "Whenever we go to the fair, we buy it. It's a once-a-year treat."

Sarah ate a couple more bites. "That's really sweet. Think I'd better quit eating, or I'll get sick."

"Let's keep moving." Ezra started walking down the midway, nibbling the cotton candy until they reached the end of the road. "Let's head to the barns and see if the judging is over."

He offered Sarah the last bite of cotton candy. She shook her head.

He popped the rest in his mouth and threw the stick into a garbage barrel sitting along the midway.

Sarah walked alongside Ezra as they entered the first barn and sauntered over to a pigpen. She wrinkled her nose at the barn's odor and swatted at a fly that buzzed near her face.

Ezra leaned over a fence. "The fair judge looks for leanness and muscling." He pointed to the hog and glanced at Sarah and David. "The back-fat depth of a show hog is ideally less than for a commercial hog." He patted the animal. "They want to see deep loin muscle."

Ezra explained the strict regimen it took to raise the animals. His *kinner* nodded. David asked a couple of questions and Ezra patiently answered. Sarah smiled as she listened to him teach his *bu*. He was a good *daed*, a kind man, and he'd make some woman a *wunderbaar ehemann*. She just wasn't sure that woman was her.

Sarah watched a couple of *buwe* who she guessed hadn't shown their animals yet. They scrubbed the hogs with a brush and water, rinsed and repeated. When water splashed her way, she stepped back and onto the foot of the person standing directly behind her.

She whirled around, swishing her hands over her dress to brush the water off. "I'm so sorry. I didn't know..." She stopped in her tracks and gazed into Caleb's eyes.

Caleb's gut clenched as he gawked at Sarah, and Ezra Smith standing next to her. The shock of seeing them together sent his heart racing until he gained control.

Ezra held out his hand. "Nice to see you, Caleb. Are you enjoying the fair?"

He swallowed hard. "*Jah*. Very much." *Until now.*

"Why didn't you come to the fair with us?" Jacob ran to Sarah and hugged her.

"She is with another friend, Jacob." Caleb gently pulled his *sohn* to his side.

"But Daed..."

"Hush, Jacob. Adults are talking." Jacob pressed his lips in a straight line.

Ezra's gaze bounced from Caleb to Sarah. "Do you two know each other?"

Caleb noticed the blush rising on Sarah's cheeks. "*Jah*, from the bakery. Mornin', Sarah."

"She's a *wunderbaar* baker." Ezra smiled down at Sarah with a twinkle in his eye.

"*Jah*, she is indeed. I promised Jacob and Mary we'd head to the horse barn next. Have a *gut* time at the fair, Sarah."

Mary glanced from Sarah to Ezra, turned to Caleb and raised a questioning brow.

"But Daed, I want to stay with Sarah."

"Sorry, Jacob, but we have a tight schedule to keep before our driver returns." He gave a firm tug on Jacob's arm and headed toward the horse barn. When they were finally out of sight, he released Jacob's arm.

"Why didn't we ask Sarah to come with us to

the fair?" Jacob sniffled. "I want her to have fun with us."

"I'm sorry. I didn't think of it." Sarah had been honest with him. Yet he hadn't imagined seeing them together would hurt so much, as though a bull were goring him and ripping his heart out. He gulped a breath of air.

He hurried his *kinner* along until they were safely in the horse barn. They visited every stall. Usually, this was the best part of the fair for Caleb, but today the joy of the judging had gone flat, like a popped bubble. "It's getting late. We need to move on."

They entered the 4-H building and walked around, viewing the project winners of horticulture, gardening, crafts and baking. Ugh. The cakes reminded Caleb of Sarah and all the memories they'd made together. Heat crept up his neck and onto his cheeks. His face burned at the thought… of her…with Ezra.

Caleb put a hand on Jacob's back and tried to push him along. The *bu* sulked, with his arms crossed in front, and dragged his feet in the dirt as he walked. Occasionally, he'd kick a rock or stick in his path. He'd let Jacob down. "Jacob, how about some saltwater taffy? *Jah?*"

A smile played at the corners of the *bu*'s mouth as if he might be fighting it, but the charm of the soft, tasty candy was too much to resist.

He allowed Jacob to select the flavor—a bag of assortments: vanilla, banana, peppermint, strawberry, orange and licorice. After he paid, Caleb whirled around just in time to catch a glimpse of Ezra and Sarah heading their way. He quickly steered Jacob and Mary in the opposite direction. His heart was shredded to pieces.

When they neared a food stand, his stomach growled at the greasy aroma. "How about a burger and some lemonade?" Mary nodded and Jacob's smile reached from ear to ear.

Caleb took a bite of his burger, but could barely get it down. He had little appetite, but Jacob seemed to have completely forgotten about Sarah. He wished he could do the same.

He glanced at his pocket watch and relief washed over him. "It's time to meet our driver." Weaving through the crowd on the midway, Caleb led the way around people entering through the front gate as they maneuvered to get out.

On the way home in the car, he heard Mary and Jacob in the back seat, crinkling the saltwater taffy paper and reminiscing about the fair with candy stuffed in their mouths, muffling their speech. The driver had his country music station cranked up, listening to the top one hundred songs in the country. *Danki, Lord.* The loud music meant he didn't have to hold a conversation. That suited Caleb just fine. His heart was still turning cartwheels at the sight of Sarah and Ezra together.

If he couldn't offer her a proposal of marriage, he had to step aside. Yet losing her gnawed at the edges of his soul.

When they finally arrived back at the farm, the *kinner* raced for the house, and Caleb traipsed to the barn to do chores. As he started preparations for milking, Tiger and her kittens scurried around underfoot.

"Shoo, Tiger. You're not getting any milk." He waved his hand in a swishing movement. They scattered, no doubt sensing the agitation brewing in his gut.

Lord, why did You put Sarah in my life if You were only going to take her away again? He didn't know what his future held, but it appeared that Sarah wasn't part of God's plan for his life.

The next morning, Caleb forced himself awake from a nightmare he was having about losing Sarah. He jumped out of bed, ate and stayed busy weeding vegetables, repairing farm equipment and preparing his numb heart for a life without Sarah. When he finished his chores, he hung the tools on a hook in the barn and headed for the house. He stopped and gazed around the farm, at the *haus*, barn, garden and out across the field. This was his world, and he'd started envisioning Sarah sitting with him on the porch in a rocker someday, sipping lemonade and making plans for the future. A lump lodged in his throat.

He tromped across the grass, toward the porch.

He glanced over his shoulder at Tiger and her kittens following behind.

Jacob ran out of the house and skidded to a stop in front of him. "Daed, when is Sarah coming to visit again? I want to show her how much the kittens have grown."

"Sarah is very busy running her bakery."

Jacob's eyes widened and a smile stretched across his mouth and lit up his face. "*Jah.* Can we go to Kalona and visit her? I'd like a brownie."

"I'm busy today—maybe another day."

The happy glow slid from Jacob's face. He crossed the barnyard, his shoulders slumped and the cats parading behind him all the way to the barn.

He hated to disappoint Jacob again, but he couldn't face Sarah just yet. What would he say to her?

As he reached the house, he felt guilty that he hadn't asked Sarah to the fair, and likewise that he'd refused to take Jacob to see his friend.

Maybe a cupcake would taste *gut* right about now…

* * *

Sarah peered up as the door opened, sending a blast of warm air throughout the bakery. "*Ach,* it's *gut* to see you all."

Ezra and his two *kinner* strolled to the counter. He motioned to the baked goods. "You can have one treat each."

They each pointed to a cookie and Sarah placed them in separate bags. She handed David the chocolate chip and Beth the sugar cookie.

Hannah teased the *kinner* by holding out a tray of candy to them. They looked at their *daed* frowning at them, then back at Hannah and shook their heads.

When Ezra wasn't looking, Hannah took two pieces of candy and plopped one in each of their sacks. "Would you like a glass of fresh lemonade to drink at the table?" she asked loudly, to cover the sound of rustling sacks.

They smiled and nodded.

Sarah got a kick out of watching her friend interact with the *kinner*. She'd make a *wunderbaar mamm*. Hopefully, someday, a *gut* man would sweep Hannah off her feet.

"I think I can get two more cookies to go along with the drinks," Hannah whispered.

David's eyes widened.

Ezra stood at the opposite end of the display case, looking at the pie, but kept stealing glances at Hannah. He looked up at Sarah and pointed to a piece of cherry pie. "And a glass of lemonade."

"Have a seat. I'll bring it to the table." Sarah cut a slice of pie and fixed a plate of assorted cookies while Hannah put five glasses of lemonade on a tray. They carried the refreshments to the table for a much-deserved break.

When Sarah finished her lemonade, she walked toward the open window. "The breeze feels like a kiss of fall. I could stand here all day."

When the *kinner* were finished, Hannah coaxed them to the counter to try cookie samples.

"Ezra." Sarah brushed the crumbs from her cookie onto her napkin and placed it in her empty paper cup. "I'm sorry, but I only want a platonic relationship."

He looked away, then back at her. "*Jah*. Okay."

Ezra didn't seem too upset. Maybe that explained his stolen looks at her friend. Hannah was a lovely woman.

The sound of hooves on the pavement drew Sarah's attention to a buggy pulling up out front. "Time for us to get back to work. Have a *gut* day, Ezra."

"*Jah*. You, too." His *kinner* followed Ezra out the door just as an older Amish couple entered.

Sarah waited on the customers. When they left, she started to clean up while Hannah packaged day-old cookies a dozen to a bag. "You didn't even snitch a cookie to eat."

"Nein." Hannah shook her head. "I'm faithful to my diet. I've lost twenty pounds and two dress sizes, and plan to lose twenty more."

"I think Ezra noticed. He was stealing glances at you."

"Nein. He's here to see you."

"We are only friends. I've made that very clear to him."

"You didn't do that with Alvin."

"Alvin was different. I don't think it would have made any difference with him. But Ezra is a kind man, with sweet *kinner.*"

The door burst open and Jacob ran in ahead of Caleb and Mary. He enveloped Sarah in a hug, then Hannah. "Why don't you come out to the farm anymore? Tiger and her kittens miss you."

"I bet the kittens are getting big." She measured out a distance with her hands.

He shook his head. "Bigger."

"Jacob." Caleb flashed his warning expression. Apparently he wasn't supposed to have asked her to visit.

The *bu* nodded, then scampered to the front of the display case. "Tiger is teaching them to be *gut* mousers like her."

"Ah. *Datt* is *wunderbaar*," Hannah chimed in.

Caleb quietly browsed the display case, his

back stiff and his shoulders squared. *Jah*, Jacob must have pestered him to come.

"Everything smells so *gut*." Jacob looked around and his eyes locked onto his favorite. "Mmm. Chocolate chip cookies."

"I will get you all a cookie and lemonade." Hannah filled plastic cups with the ice-cold beverage and dotted a plate with an assortment of cookies.

Sarah meandered over by Mary. "Let me know when you're ready to can again, and I'll help."

"*Danki* but Aent Lillia said she'd help me next time." Mary kept her gaze focused on the shelves of sweets.

"That's nice." Only, Sarah wanted to be the one to help her. She was hurt by the rejection, but a thought occurred to her. Maybe Caleb felt rejected when he saw her with Ezra at the fair, and that was the reason for his standoffish attitude.

Hannah set the tray with the lemonade on a table. The *kinner* sat down and each took a cookie.

Sarah waited while Caleb stared at the baked goods, but the silence stretched into awkwardness. *Jah*, his feelings must be hurt. She'd tried to spare him by telling him about Ezra, but obviously she'd handled that badly. She shouldn't have gone to the fair with Ezra and his *kinner*.

"The cinnamon-raisin bread looks *gut*." His words almost sounded like he choked them out.

"It is. Very *gut*. Hannah made it."

He lifted his eyes and met her gaze. She leaned over the counter. "Caleb, I'm sorry if I made things difficult between us. I told you the bishop had his matchmaking hat on. Ezra and I are just friends." The thought of sitting next to Caleb in the buggy flashed through her mind, followed by the horrific idea that if he believed their relationship was threatened, he might abandon it.

Caleb shuffled his feet a step closer to the counter and swiped a hand down his beard. "Sarah, I understand. You *should* accept invitations. We don't have a commitment. When I saw you there with Ezra, it took me by surprise, that's all. I hadn't planned to bump into you at the fair."

She walked around the counter and stood next to him. Her heart drummed wildly in her chest at his nearness.

He stammered. "Sarah, would you like to attend Sunday school again with me sometime?"

"*Jah.* I look forward to going."

Chapter Fifteen

The bakery door opened, interrupting Sarah's scrubbing of the display case. *Ach*, it was almost closing and the few remaining baked goods were in the cooler. She raised her shoulders and gasped when she saw her brother. "Turner, why the serious face? Something wrong?"

"Come sit with me. I need to talk to you." He scrubbed his hands over his face before facing Sarah. "I hate to do this."

"What is it?" She sensed something dreadful had happened. "Is it Aent Emma?" She'd already had one heart attack.

He leaned forward in his chair, shook his head solemnly, braced his elbows on the table and intertwined his fingers together under his chin.

"Is this about Caleb Brenneman?" Fear seized her heart.

"Nein." Turner dropped both hands so they

hit the table palms down and made a loud thud. "Sarah, I've sold the bakery, all the contents and the name. I've signed the purchase agreement and will sign final papers next week, in the lawyer's office."

Her mouth dropped open, and a loud cry escaped before her hand covered her mouth. A cold numbness slowly consumed her body.

When the shock subsided, she lowered her hand. "I can't believe you sold the bakery out from under me." Sweat clung to her palms.

"I didn't want to. But Naomi is pregnant and the apartment above the woodworking shop is dusty, noisy and no place to raise a *boppli*. The money from the sale of the bakery will go toward building a house. This old bakery and structure won't bring much, probably just enough to build a small, modest *haus*."

"Then why sell it when you know it means so much to me? I have to support myself. You're putting me out on the street."

"I thought you and Ezra Smith were getting married. People saw you at the fair together. You missed your chance with Alvin."

"Unbelievable," Sarah snapped at him. "Do you *liebe* Naomi?"

"Of course I do. What does that have to do with this?"

"You and Naomi are madly in *liebe* with each

other. But you thought I should marry Alvin, a man I dislike, and take care of him, his *haus* and his six *kinner*."

"You would have grown to *liebe* him like Mamm and Daed. Theirs was an arranged marriage."

She gasped. "How long do I have before I have to move out?"

"You have thirty days from next Monday."

"Is he buying all of the ovens and the pans that Mamm and Daed originally had in the bakery?"

"*Jah.* You should have them and the shop all cleaned by his possession date."

"I'll let you know when I'm moving." She pushed her chair away from the table, her eyes averted from Turner, and stomped to the door. "*Danki* for giving me notice, Turner. Now please leave. I have a lot of thinking, planning and packing to do."

"Listen, Sarah." He made his way to the front door. "Don't be so huffy. It's time you remarried anyway."

"You don't have the right to tell me when to get remarried and neither does the bishop. Was this his idea?"

"Of course not. He had nothing to do with this. Our faith requires that a woman think about her family, church and community before herself."

"*Danki* for the reminder. I know the sacrifice

women must make, Turner. I'll tell you right now, I'm not marrying a man I don't *liebe* or care for just to have a roof over my head. Please leave. I have things to do."

She locked the door, turned out the lights in the front and made her wobbly legs carry her to the back of the bakery. Hannah stood in the middle of the kitchen floor, her mouth open and tears rolling down her cheeks. Sarah rushed into her friend's waiting arms.

Hannah rubbed her back soothingly. "What are you going to do? You can come and stay at our farm. Mamm and Daed would love to have you."

Sarah stepped back and wiped the tears from her cheeks. "I need to think about it. I'm going to be open for a couple more days to say goodbye to our customers. They have been faithful, and I want to thank them. Go home, Hannah. We'll talk tomorrow. I'm exhausted and my heart is ripped in two. I can't even think right now."

The pity in Hannah's eyes sliced through her every bit as much as Turner's words. Sarah was grateful that he had let her live here and operate the bakery as long as she had. She just hadn't prepared herself for the day he exercised his right to sell.

Wandering throughout the bakery, Sarah swiped her hand across the stove, touched the counters and cabinets. She caressed the Best

Bakery wall plaque with her fingertips. Daed had received it from the town for giving away baked goods to charity. Sarah remembered all the fun her family had had here. Not just work, but laughing and talking about the future. Her chest swelled with pain.

Since she was a small girl, she'd watched her parents work in the bakery. The recipes never existed on paper, to avoid theft. They'd taught Sarah each recipe, and she had tucked them away in her memory. The Amish Sweet Delights bakery was a favorite tourist attraction in the Kalona area. Now all that her parents had worked for was gone.

She tried to drink in all the memories. How had the new owner seen inside the bakery? Had he come in and bought something? Turner had a key. He must have let him in when she'd closed for the night. Would Turner have done that?

Jah, he must have.

She crossed her arms in front of her and stared out the window, into the darkening sky, into the unknown. What did Daed constantly quip when she'd fallen and skinned a knee? *Buck up, you're tougher than that, tochter.*

Nein home and *nein* prospect of a job kept spinning around in her head. She had some money saved up. Turner hadn't charged her rent, so her savings had grown into a tidy sum, and she had money from the sale of her and Samuel's small *haus*.

The queasiness in her stomach overwhelmed her for a moment. Maybe she'd hook up King and take a drive in the country to clear her head.

She knew the Amish custom—girls married, the older boys were given money to start a business and the youngest boy inherited the property. In her family's case, Turner had been the only *sohn*. She just never thought he'd sell the bakery out from under her. Not Mamm and Daed's bakery. The bakery was part of her soul like a family homestead.

It was hard to believe that her *bruder* actually expected her to marry someone she didn't *liebe*.

Sarah drew in a deep breath, locked the back door and trudged up the stairs to her apartment. To make a plan…for her future.

After Daed's death, she unquestioningly took over managing the bakery. She wandered over to her sitting room window, laid her hand over the back of Daed's rocker and gave it a push. He often rocked in the chair when he had a problem to ponder. She smoothed the back of her skirt as she sat in the chair.

What was she going to do? There was an empty building in Kalona, next to the Knit 'n' Sew shop. She could call the Realtor and ask to walk through it. To open a new shop in town meant competing with her old bakery. Since Amish Sweet Delights was in the Kalona tourism guide, they would get most of the tourist business. The town only redid the guidebooks every few years. Could she even compete with Amish Sweet Delights? She usually talked to Turner when she had a problem. Not this time.

She changed into a fresh dress, hitched King to her buggy and headed for the country. To clear her mind and, like Daed would say, reseed. She had to move on, figure out where to go, what to do next…for the rest of her life.

Caleb opened the door. "What a delightful surprise, Sarah. Come in."

"*Nein.* Would you mind coming out and sitting on your porch so we can talk privately?"

He closed the door and escorted her to the porch swing he'd made. "Something wrong?"

She filled him in on Turner's visit and the sale of the bakery. "Turner had the right," she emphasized. Her voice broke twice but she made it through telling him about their conversation.

He wrapped his arm around her shoulders and squeezed. "What are your plans? Where will you live?"

"Hannah said I could stay with her and her folks."

"You're a *wunderbaar* baker. You could work for someone else, maybe even the new owner."

"*Nein.* I won't do that."

"Okay. I understand. Rent a shop or buy a building and start a new bakery?"

"If I opened a regular bakery, the commercial ovens each would cost between five and twenty thousand. I would also need a cooler and display case." Her hands fidgeted in her lap and pulled at a loose thread in the hem of her apron. "Guess I'm scared of failing."

"Everyone loves your baking."

"*Jah*, but I'd have to compete with Amish Sweet Delights. Turner sold the name, along with the bakery and its contents. Therefore, my bakery reputation will not follow me. My local customers may come back. Tourism creates a huge boost to sales. But the tourists visit the bakery listed in the tour books and brochures. The town only updates and reprints the tourism books every few years."

He turned toward her as much as he could in the swing. "I can help you hunt for a *haus* or shop and lend you money."

"*Danki.* But I don't need your money. I just wanted to get out of the bakery and think. We're open Monday and Tuesday, maybe Wednesday. I want to say goodbye to our loyal customers."

"If you start your own business, I know you'll succeed." He covered her hand with his and squeezed.

"*Danki* for the encouragement." A weak smile tugged at her mouth.

Caleb couldn't imagine a *bruder* doing that to his unmarried sister, even if he did have the right. He couldn't ask Sarah to marry him. At least not yet.

Something about this woman brought out his protective nature. But what else could he do to help Sarah?

Sarah gazed out over Caleb's farm and drew a deep breath. She'd bared her soul to this man. He was a sweetheart to listen while she unloaded her burden. His encouragement, his strength and his confidence seeped through her. Uplifted her.

She hoped he hadn't judged Turner. He was her *bruder,* and she would *liebe* him according to *Gott*'s will. She understood that property went to the youngest male of the family. The bakery was his to do with as he wished. She would not harbor ill thoughts of him.

Caleb was a safe refuge while *Gott* was letting her wander. She blotted a tear in the corner of her eye with her fingertip. Like Moses in the desert, she had to figure out what *Gott*'s will was for her life.

"What do you think you will do?" She could sense Caleb measuring his words. Was an idea going through his head? Maybe a marriage proposal. *Nein*, he wasn't ready for a commitment yet.

"I'm thinking about renting a *haus* in Kalona and putting in a home bakery. I reviewed the laws, and it is fortunate that I live in Iowa. It is one of the few states that allow home bakeries. I'm just limited to the amount the home bakery can earn. Still, I can gauge if I'll get enough business to open a bakery here in town." She rested her head on Caleb's arm, lying over the back of the swing.

Caleb tapped her arm. "What would you call a new bakery?"

She leveled her gaze at him and tried to smile. The idea appealed to her the more she talked about it. "I hadn't really thought about it—maybe Sweet Daed's."

"I like it." His sage-green eyes sparkled as he nodded.

They swung back and forth in silence a few minutes. Her heart swelled with *liebe* and appreciation for Caleb. He was a *gut* soul mate, with a listening ear. He sprinkled in just the right amount of advice and sweetened it with encouragement. His arm wrapped her in warmth, while his strength penetrated deep into her heart and spirit.

She let out a long sigh. *It's in* Gott*'s hands. He apparently has a new direction for my life.*

Straightening her back, she lifted her chin. After the shock of Samuel's death and Turner selling the bakery, she had never been more ready to get on with her life than now.

Chapter Sixteen

Monday dawned with a brilliant sun forcing its way through angry gray clouds. Sarah took that as an encouraging reminder from *Gott* that He can do great things. She wiped the bakery's chalkboard clean and wrote a notice along with the daily special.

Bakery sold. New owner to take over Amish Sweet Delights on September 1. Today through Wednesday, FREE coffee with the purchase of any one item.

She unlocked the door and flipped the sign to Open.

Within minutes, the first customer entered and stood in front of the sign. "I'll miss your bakery, and my husband will miss your cinnamon rolls. He takes one every day to work and eats it on break."

"*Danki.* I'm sad about leaving, but Turner owned the bakery and decided to sell."

Later in the morning, she overheard a couple of jean-clad customers grumbling about Turner selling the shop out from under her. *Jah*, the gossip had started. She pretended not to hear but could detect the mood in the bakery had turned somber.

She pasted on a smile. By noon, it became harder to mask her breaking heart. When the doorbell jingled, Caleb's gaze met hers. His wink of encouragement and his smiling face boosted her morale and warmed her spirit.

Jacob followed close behind his *daed* and hugged her with tear-filled eyes. "Daed said you sold the bakery and this was your last week. I can't come to see you anymore or work for you?" His voice quivered.

"Of course you can. I just won't be here, in *this* shop. When I move, I will need your help."

"Where will you be?"

She glanced up and noticed the patrons at the tables were watching her and undoubtedly listening to their conversation. "I'll let you know when I move. I have a surprise for you," she whispered. "You can have anything in the bakery. It's on the house."

"What does that mean?" he whispered back.

"It's free because you are my special friend. Your *daed* can have a free cup of coffee if he buys something." She glanced at Caleb.

He raised an eyebrow. "I'm not a special friend?"

She smiled.

Caleb pointed to a cinnamon roll. "How are you doing? Have you made plans yet?"

Sarah pulled the roll out of the case, placed it on a plate and poured his coffee. "*Jah*. I'll spend the next week here cleaning and getting it ready for the new owner. After that, I'm moving into a *haus* I've rented here in town and will start a small bakery. The drawback is a home bakery can only earn twenty thousand dollars a year." She flashed him a broad smile. "I was hoping you'd help me move."

"*Jah*, just let me know when."

She squared her shoulders. "There's a peace in me that *Gott* is leading me down a different road and into a new chapter of my life. Strangely, when I updated the bakery chalkboard this morning, a thread of excitement wove through my veins about this new journey. I'm actually getting anxious to see where His Spirit leads me. I thought *Gott* had abandoned me. But maybe He waited until He'd softened my heart and curbed my stubbornness before I could take the next step in my life."

A little guilt tugged at his gut. After Sarah settled into her *haus*, he needed to approach her about changing to New Order. Now she had enough dealing with the bakery. He didn't want to upset her with another big change. Not just yet, anyway.

Sarah waited on everyone in line at the counter. When she snagged a break, she wandered to the tables with the carafe of coffee, refilled cups and sat by Jacob and Caleb for a minute.

Jacob threw his arms around Sarah. "Don't move too far away, please. I will miss you too much." Moisture pooled in the corner of his eye.

Sarah held him tightly. It was her worst fear that she'd have to leave Jacob when she couldn't find a vacant shop. "I'm renting a *haus* in Kalona so I'll be nearby," she whispered. His body stopped trembling. He relaxed his shoulders and blinked back a tear.

"Can I help you pack?" His tiny voice quivered.

"Of course. Hannah and I could use your strong arms."

Jacob held his right arm up, bent it at the elbow and flexed his bicep.

"Wow," Hannah gasped as she approached from the kitchen door. "You are strong."

Jacob laughed and nodded as he put his arm down. "I do a lot of farm work."

"I have some business in town on Saturday. I'll drop Jacob off in the morning," Caleb offered.

When the doorbell sprung to life, she headed back to the counter, and Caleb and Jacob waved on their way out the door. A pang of sadness squeezed Sarah's chest as they walked out of the Amish Sweet Delights bakery for the last time.

Tuesday was double the business of Monday. Every chance Sarah had, she ran back to the kitchen and helped Hannah with the baking.

Wednesday tugged on her heart—her last day to have the bakery. Tears blurred her vision for the whole eight hours. "Hannah, the past three days we've had more business than we've generally have in six days. There hasn't been this much business since Daed was alive."

Hannah nodded in agreement. "It feels like your *daed* died all over again."

"*Jah.* It touches my soul to witness how the community appreciated the bakery." She had helped Hannah bake all day to keep up with sales.

At 5:00 p.m., Sarah closed the front door, locked it and flipped the sign for the last time. A chill swept over her.

Her parents' legacy…gone.

Her dream…gone.

Tears ran down her cheeks and dripped off her

chin. She reached for the counter to steady her step. Hannah ran from the back of the bakery, wrapped her arms around Sarah, and held her until she quit sobbing and shaking.

"I'm okay, Hannah. *Danki* for being my friend and helping me all these years."

Tears welled up, but she blinked them back. Tomorrow, she'd set her feet on a new path.

Sarah awoke in the middle of the night with a to-do list whirling in her head. She sat up and reached for the flashlight on the bed stand. Her loose hair tumbled off her shoulders, fell past her waist and rested on the bed. She pulled her hair to her left and drew it over her shoulder so it wouldn't catch when she leaned back. *Ach, Lord, my long hair is an outward symbol of submission to You. But it does get in the way sometimes.*

She plucked her prayer book from the drawer of her nightstand, took out the marker and settled back. After reading only a couple of pages, her mind drifted back to the tasks that needed to be done before she moved. Returning her book to the drawer, she rummaged in the back until she found a pad and pencil. She jotted down boxes, twine, cleaning products, then wrote down what cleaning she'd already done and what remained for her to do. Her brain raced from one thing to another, pushing sleep out of her head.

She reviewed the lists. She'd pack away some of her own pans that she wouldn't need until she started her own bakery and noted that in another column.

Sarah glanced at the clock. It was now 3:00 a.m. She rubbed her forehead to clear the fog out of her brain, but it didn't help. Maybe a short break would refresh her mind. She rested her head back against the headboard.

Ringing blasted in her ears and roused her from a deep slumber. She reached over and hit the alarm button. A glance at her to-do list propelled her out of bed. She threw her dress on, pinned her hair up in a bun, slid on her prayer *kapp* and headed to the bakery.

Sarah scooped medium-roast into the coffee maker, added water and started the brewer. She glanced around at the chaos of boxes and cleaning products, but the idea of owning her own bakery boosted her energy level. Stuff she considered hers, she started packing in cartons and pushing to the side.

The back door opened and closed. "Is the coffee hot?" Hannah shivered. "It's chilly out there."

"Hot and strong. Your cup is ready."

Hannah gave her a hug. "How're ya doing today?"

"Better."

Hannah pulled a chair away from the table and

collapsed into her usual morning heap. "Thanks for having my coffee ready."

"I made a list of things I had to do this morning. That was on it."

Sarah poured a mug of brew for herself and sat at the table. She took a couple of sips and cradled the mug in her hands. Glancing around the bakery, her heart felt as empty as the pantry. How was it going to feel not coming here every day?

The bakery her folks had cherished would belong to someone else. Everything that was familiar. Gone.

Well, almost.

Since Mamm and Daed's recipes didn't exist in written form, the new owner wouldn't get those. She set the mug down. Surely Turner couldn't make her write them down. Could he?

The front door whooshed open and closed as Jacob entered. "What happened to the bell?"

Sarah swallowed a gulp of coffee. "I took it down and packed it."

Jacob hung his hat on a peg and tossed her a sympathetic smile. The little *bu* had a way of sprinkling her day with sunshine even when it rained.

Sarah motioned to the stacked pots and pans, then to the cartons. "You can pack all those pans, Jacob." He set to work and packed five cartons before his *daed* stopped to pick him up.

Jacob wrapped her in hug and Sarah sensed by his squeeze that he felt her grief through the anguish of losing his *mamm*. A *bu* still grieving his *mamm*'s death understood her pain. She laid her head on his tiny shoulder and blinked back a tear.

Caleb wrapped them both in a hug. "Do you need anything?"

She shook her head. All she really needed was these two in her life. With their love and encouragement, she could deal with losing her bakery.

Sarah wandered through her rented *haus,* trying to imagine living here. She'd lost the bakery, the one place she'd called home. Tomorrow was moving day. Her life, like stale cake, was crumbling.

After cleaning the cupboards, flooring and walls, Sarah returned to her apartment. She unhitched King and walked up the sidewalk, admiring the yellow and gold chrysanthemums that waved in the warm fall breeze in the garden her *daed* had started. Sarah headed upstairs, pulled out some empty boxes and packed the last of her possessions.

At bedtime, images of being alone the rest of her life ran through her mind for hours. The bakery had given her life a purpose. But now? A hollowness settled in her heart.

Sarah lay in bed with her life seemingly out of

her reach, like the tiny star shining through the window. She stared into the darkness and closed her eyes.

Dawn crept into the room until Sarah forced her sleep-deprived eyes open, heaved her body out of bed, dressed and wandered down to the bakery for one last goodbye. Her heart pounded while her eyes fought back tears. She unlocked the door and stepped in for the last time.

Sarah roamed around the kitchen, soaking up the essence of the past, sliding her hand over the cupboard doors that gaped open to air the scrubbed shelves. The aroma of Lysol and ammonia still hung in the air and stung her eyes.

She walked out of the bakery and locked the door for the last time.

Now she had to trust *Gott*.

Chapter Seventeen

Caleb's footfalls echoed in the empty room as he inspected the paint job he'd done on Sarah's rented *haus*. The cream color she'd selected for the kitchen reflected the sunlight and brightened her work area. The bedroom's pale yellow walls cast a cheery glow about the room. She'd appreciate that. Where was she, anyway?

He searched upstairs, and wound his way through the first floor to the kitchen. She wasn't downstairs either. He peered out the window. Sarah sat forlornly on the back stoop, elbows propped on her knees, with hands clasped under her chin. She looked deep in thought.

Caleb stepped down off the stoop and sat next to her. "You okay?"

"I will be." Her voice wavered. "I feel as empty as the house."

He wrapped his arm around her and pulled her close.

She leaned her head against his shoulder. "I appreciate all your help and support, Caleb." She laid her hand on his and squeezed. The warmth of her soft skin felt good against his. His heart swelled with *liebe*. He wanted to take away her hurt, but he had no words that would do that.

Caleb recognized the squeaking breaks of the *Englischer*'s truck they had loaded her belongings in, and heard it pull into her drive. "Ezra and his friend are here."

She nodded and sat up straight. "*Danki* for asking them to move my furniture."

The sensation of her scooting away from him sent a lonely shiver through his body. He could multiply that feeling by a thousand if she moved to another town.

Caleb stood and helped Sarah to her feet. He placed his hand on her back as she stepped up on the stoop. His heart twisted tighter and tighter with *liebe* for this woman. Ever since he'd seen her with Ezra at the fair, he couldn't keep from thinking about her, dreaming of her. Worrying about losing her.

But he couldn't ask her to marry him until Mary accepted the idea and Sarah agreed to change to New Order. And he couldn't ask her to do that when she'd just lost her bakery.

He opened the back door for Sarah. "I'll go help unload the truck."

When they entered the kitchen, she headed toward the coffee pot. "I'll have coffee and sandwiches for all of you when you're done. The boxes are marked. I'll be there in a minute to guide the furniture to its place."

They worked all morning, bringing in boxes, crates and furniture, creating a maze of passages. Little by little, the mess disappeared as she directed each piece of furniture to its rightful spot. By noon the *haus* looked great, and she could spend the night in her own bed.

After Ezra and his friend left, Caleb helped her move furniture and uncrate furnishings. While she washed dishes and put them away, he hung a coatrack, tightened a doorknob and attached her spice cabinet above the stove.

The next morning, Sarah finished unpacking her clothes and placed the linens in the upstairs closet. Her next task was to tackle the mess in the kitchen. She pushed the labyrinth of boxes to make a path from the table to the stove. She plopped her hands on her hips, looked around and cringed at the mountain of work left to do.

The sudden knock on the front door startled her. It sounded like a tapping. Were there woodpeckers around?

She hurried through the maze of cartons and flung the door open. *"Ach."* Sarah's lip quivered at the sight of her friends. Caleb, and Jacob, standing next to Hannah. "I'm so glad to see you. Come in."

"Hope you don't mind, but Jacob insisted on coming to help you unpack boxes. I'll help, too, after I run an errand." Caleb said as he took a step back toward his buggy.

"Of course we can use Jacob's help," Hannah responded. "That tool belt he is wearing will come in handy today. We will get a full day's use of him."

"I'm ready to start right away." Jacob slid his hammer out of his tool belt and held it up. "It's *gut* for knocking on doors, too." A mischievous smile spread across his face. "Did you get a dog, Sarah. There is one lying under the tree?"

"*Nein*, that is my dog, Mint-Candy. He followed me to work." Hannah shook her head. "He's a lazy dog and will sleep all day until I go home."

Sarah chuckled as Jacob and Hannah talked and followed her inside. She pointed to the boxes marked Kitchen. "While I clean and arrange the pantry, if you two could unpack, wash and arrange the dishes in the cupboards, I would greatly appreciate it."

They worked all morning. Jacob found a loose handle on a drawer. He pulled his Phillips screwdriver out of his belt, gave the screw a few twists and a grunt at the final turn.

"Good job," Hannah praised, and Jacob's face beamed.

Sarah's throat tightened at the way this little *bu* bloomed when encouraged. "Who has an idea for a name for our new home bakery? I had thought about Sweet Daed's, but I'm open to other suggestions."

Silence ruled the kitchen as thought waves flew around, dodging an occasional pan banging.

Jacob brushed his hands across his trousers. "I could think better if I had a cookie to eat."

"You could, huh. Help yourself." Hannah chuckled, "So, that's the problem with these hips. I am thinking too much."

Sarah stifled a laugh while listening to the two of them banter.

Jacob stuck his hand in the cookie jar and retrieved a large chocolate chunk cookie. He took a bite. "I have it!" Crumbs flew from his mouth as he spoke. "Let's call it The Cookie Box."

"I *liebe* it." Hannah chuckled.

Sarah gasped. "Me, too. That's it. We'll need to advertise. Maybe post some flyers around town. Hannah, ask your friend to make us some posters to tack around town, and a web page."

"*Gut* idea." Hannah poured three glasses of lemonade and pulled three cookies from the jar. "We need to celebrate first." They cleared a spot on the table, held their glasses up and clinked them together. "To The Cookie Box."

Sarah grabbed a pad and pencil. "Let's get started. We need to apply for the license and get an inspection. I'll ask Caleb to build us some tables and racks for our baked goods."

On opening day, Sarah hung the *Welkum* sign and unlocked the dead bolt on the kitchen door of The Cookie Box. She turned and squealed. "We're open!"

Hannah embraced her friend. "It's all ours." She whirled Sarah around in a circle, like she had when they were girls.

"Stop, Hannah, I'm getting dizzy." Sarah plopped into a chair to catch her breath. "I can't believe how *gut* it feels to own a bakery again, even if it's only part-time."

Horses' hooves and buggy wheels churned to a stop in front of the *haus,* indicating the bakery might have its first customers. Sarah stood and took a quick glance around to make sure everything was ready.

Melinda Miller opened the door and strolled in with a smile stretching across her face. "I'm so glad you're open for business, Sarah. I've sure missed buying my bread at your bakery." She took a deep breath. "Mmm. It smells delicious in here. Two loaves of whole wheat and one white bread."

Sarah smiled. "It's good to see you, Melinda. *Danki* for supporting us." She bagged up her order and before she was through, two more customers had walked in and were looking around.

By the end of the day, several of their old customers had stopped in and made purchases. Sarah hadn't been sure how much they needed to bake for The Cookie Box. As it turned out, the guess was a *gut* one.

Peeking out the window at closing time, Hannah watched the last person drive away. "Yeah! We got several of our old customers back."

Sarah twirled around with her arms in the air. "We did." She scooted to the coffee pot, poured two cups and handed Hannah hers. Sarah held her cup in the air.

Hannah clinked her cup to the other. "I'm happy for you, Sarah. The bakery's going to be a big success."

A loud knock caught their attention. Hannah nodded toward the door. "Go answer, Sarah, and I'll make a pie for tomorrow."

Sarah set her cup on the table, opened the door and threw her arms around Turner. "*Danki* for stopping by for our opening. I didn't expect it. Would you like a cup of coffee and a roll?"

"*Nein.*" He removed his straw hat and turned it

around in his hands. "I would like to have a private conversation with you on the porch."

She motioned to the door and followed him out. They sat in the two rocking chairs that Hannah's *daed* had made her for the porch.

"Sarah, have you been talking about me?" Her *bruder* was never one to beat around the bush.

She stared at Turner, baffled, and then stumbled for the words. "What? *Nein*. What are you talking about?"

"Since your bakery closed, my woodworking business has declined. Ken Johnson, Amish Sweet Delights' new owner, said his business also took a downturn."

Sarah didn't know quite what to say. Their businesses were declining and they blamed her. A prickly feeling inched its way up her back. "I have said nothing about you or Mr. Johnson. People make up their own minds. They don't need me to tell them what they like or dislike." She stood and propped her fists on her hips.

"If you don't have anything else to say to me, I need to get back in and help Hannah."

Turner stared at the hat in his hands and didn't reply. He stood and headed for his buggy.

She stomped into the kitchen and shoved the door closed.

Hannah looked up. "Problem?"

"He said the Amish Sweet Delights business

and his have declined since he sold the bakery and wanted to know if I've been gossiping about them." Sarah paced back and forth across the kitchen floor. "I haven't said a word."

Hannah looked up from rolling a piecrust. "Daed said there is talk in the community. People liked that you ran your *daed*'s Amish Sweet Delights and they liked your baked goods. Some have tried the new bakery and said their baked products aren't as *gut* as yours."

"Maybe if Mr. Johnson and Turner are blaming me, they have a guilty conscience," Sarah sniffed.

Hannah dumped the apples she had already cut and spiced into the pie shell and placed strips of woven dough over the top for a crust. She pinched the edges of the dough and set it in the oven. "Daed said that some folks around town, like Lazy Susan, didn't like that Amish don't make at least some of the products for the Amish Sweet Delights bakery. Susan said it makes her café and all the businesses in town look bad, like their goods aren't authentic."

Sarah stood at the opposite end of the table from Hannah. "Really? How do people know that an Amish woman is not helping with the baking?"

"Someone asked Mr. Johnson. He told them he was trying to find an Amish woman, but in the meantime, he and his wife were doing all the baking."

"Why didn't you tell me that before, Hannah?"

"For the reason you just spoke of—so Turner couldn't accuse you of starting the gossip. But he did anyway. Sorry. I should have told you earlier."

Sarah pulled a chair away from the table and sat. "I never dreamed our baked goods were *that* much better."

"We are both terrific bakers." Hannah chuckled and sat next to Sarah. "I'm still shocked Turner sold the name of the bakery."

"*Jah*, me, too. I don't even know how Turner and this man met. Turner inherited the bakery and all the contents, so it was his right to sell it and the name."

"How about the recipes?"

"Mamm and Daed never wrote them down. They taught me from memory. Turner knew that. He never baked, so he never learned them."

"Could he make you give them to Mr. Johnson?"

"I don't know. I hope not." Sarah wrung her hands.

Caleb walked across Sarah's porch. Jacob followed but bumped the door. "Quiet, Jacob. Be careful."

"Sorry, Daed. With my arms full, I lost my balance."

Caleb opened the door and poked his head in. "Mmm. Smells *wunderbaar* in here."

Sarah laughed. "What are you two up to out there? Come in."

"*Nein*, Jacob wants you and Hannah to come out. He has a surprise for you." Jacob giggled and scuffled around on the porch.

Sarah dried her hands while Hannah headed for the door. Hannah stepped out on the porch and roared with laughter. "Sarah, come see."

Caleb held the door open, his eyes feasting on every move Sarah made. She walked by cautiously with a smile pulling at the corners of her mouth.

"Oh, how cute. Tiger and her kittens have come for a visit, but Mint-Candy doesn't seem to like them."

Hannah laughed. "I'll give those cats a big dish of milk if they can get a rise out of that lazy dog. The walk over here seems to have tuckered him out."

Tiger and her kittens jumped and chased each other around the yard as if they'd never seen grass before. Mint-Candy lay in a ball, his eyelids closed. Some of the kittens nipped at his tail and others chewed on his feet. One kitty went nose to nose with Mint-Candy, but the lazy pup didn't seem to care.

"That's a funny name for a dog." Jacob patted the terrier.

"*Jah*—" Hannah scratched the dog's ears

"—there is a story behind it. When the dog was young, Daed had bought a box of mint candy. This little ball of fur climbed onto his chair and got the box of candy off the end table and ate all of them and chewed up the container. He smelled like mint for days."

Jacob laughed until he fell on the ground beside Mint-Candy.

Hannah bent down beside Jacob. "We kept calling him that and the name stuck. He likes to take naps. Don't think even a summer's storm could chase him from his spot." Hannah turned to head back into Sarah's house. "I'll bring out a pitcher of lemonade and some cookies."

Jacob laughed and played with the kittens.

Caleb motioned to Sarah. "Shall we have a seat?"

Sarah pulled out a chair by the table Hannah's *daed* had made for her porch. "What brings you two to town on a beautiful September day?"

"Errands, and I promised Mary I was going to mention to you that she plans on canning tomatoes again on Monday."

"I'll be by to help. I'm still hoping to repair the damage with Mary. At least she likes me to help her can tomatoes, so that gets me in her kitchen. Maybe I can earn her forgiveness someday."

Caleb reached over and squeezed her small hand, lying on the table. Her soft skin teased the tips of his fingers and sent a streak of warmth straight to his heart. The breeze had caught a few strands of Sarah's dark brown hair and danced them around her cinnamon-brown eyes. The soft flutter like a bow on a violin plucked at his heartstrings. If anyone could replace Martha in his heart, it was Sarah.

The thought of a commitment sent a jolt bolting through him. *Nein.* Not yet.

Chapter Eighteen

Sarah woke at dawn on Saturday determined to get an early start on baking. She stood at the sink, the sun's bright yellow beams streaming through the window while she washed a stack of pans. On the weekend, it would be nice to have Jacob's help. Maybe she'd mention it to Caleb. She missed that little *bu* and the joy he brought her.

She stirred up a batch of peanut butter cookies and glanced at Hannah, whose nose was stuck in a recipe book as she hummed a hymn from the *Ausbund*. Her friend never went this long without talking; she always had some tidbit of news to share.

Hannah zipped around the kitchen in her new dress that looked two sizes smaller than her old one. She never mentioned her additional weight loss. But Sarah suspected that Ezra stopping by every Saturday and flirting with Hannah had something to do with her good mood.

Sarah rolled the dough into walnut-sized balls, dropped them onto the baking sheets, pressed them down, popped them in the oven and set the timer. The heat from the oven made the small kitchen hot. She picked up a pot holder and fanned it past her face, but it had little effect. She poured herself a glass of lemonade and strolled out onto the porch to enjoy the warm fall day.

The breeze rustled the hem of her dress as she walked to the railing. The air blew across her skin, cooling and refreshing her. She propped one hip against the railing and looked up to heaven. *Your scripture revealed that You have a plan for us, but where's mine,* Gott? *I have no family and no future. Where do I go from here, Lord?*

Silence. Not even a bird was singing.

The timer rang. She sent a final glance heavenward, then hurried back in, pulled the cookies out of the oven and set them on a rack to cool.

At noon, Hannah's folks walked in, letting a draft from the outside follow them in. Sarah tossed the happy wanderers a smile. "*Welkum* back, Edna and John. How was the trip to Missouri, and your visit with your *sohn* and his family?"

"Oh, Sarah, what fun we had!" Edna gushed.

Hannah hugged her *mamm* and *daed*.

"Oh, you wouldn't believe what a *wunderbaar* time we had. It brought tears to my eyes to see them, and we hated to leave." Edna sat and filled them in on the trip.

"I'd like some tea and cookies," John chimed in when his wife paused. "Carrying all those suitcases upstairs was hard work."

Sarah made tea and set a plate of cookies on the table. Edna chattered, spilling the news on everyone and everything going on in Seymour, Missouri.

John wiped his brow with a hanky, took a cookie and smiled. "I longed the whole trip home for one of Hannah's cookies. No one makes a tasty *makrone*, macaroon, like her." He licked his lips.

"Hannah, dear, your father and I would like a few words with you," Edna said after she took a bite of cookie and a sip of tea.

Sarah stood. Edna's tone let her know they had a family matter to discuss. "I'll let you visit." She busied herself in another area of the *haus* until she heard Hannah's parents leave.

When Sarah entered the kitchen, Hannah's face was red and her eyes were puffy. "What's wrong?" She rushed to Hannah's side and enveloped her in a hug.

"*Jah*, everything is wrong." When a customer opened the door, Hannah stepped back from her friend. "Tell you later," she whispered.

When the last customer left, Sarah poured two glasses of lemonade and carried them to the table.

"Come and have a seat." Hannah's face looked tense, and her hand shook hard enough that the lemonade sloshed over the top.

"What is it, Hannah? You look worried. Is something wrong? Is your *mamm* or *daed* sick, or your *bruder*?"

"No one is sick. My folks are getting older, Daed's arthritic hands hurt and it makes it difficult for him to farm by himself. They are both tired of the cold and snowy Iowa winters. They want to move south to Missouri." Her voice wavered with concern. She took a sip of lemonade.

Sarah's stomach clenched as she waited for Hannah to regain control.

Hannah drew a deep breath and blew it out. "My *bruder* wants them to sell the farm, move to Seymour and live in the *dawdi-haus* on his farm."

"Ach." The gravity of Hannah's words settled over Sarah. "Are they going to move?"

Her friend twisted her glass on the table's surface, stopped, and slid her fingers up and down the condensation clinging to the outside. Hannah's brown eyes peered up and met Sarah's gaze.

"I have to move to Missouri with them, Sarah."

Hannah's words covered Sarah like a cold blanket of snow. She let the words float on the air to make sure she heard them correctly. "I see."

"I'm so sorry, Sarah. I won't be here to help you with the bakery anymore."

"*Nein.* That's okay. When do you go?"

She told Sarah all the details. "We move at the end of the year. They already have a buyer and Daed agreed to let him have the farm in December."

Sarah settled back in her chair to let the shock sink in. She hadn't expected it to be quite so soon. "I will have to find someone to replace you."

An unchecked tear rolled down Hannah's cheek. She snatched a tissue from her pocket and blotted the moisture. "I'm so sorry, Sarah."

"I know you are. Don't look so glum. It's not the apocalypse."

Hannah's laugh shook with tension. "I'm going to miss you, Sarah. I didn't want to go, but Daed said it was unacceptable for a single woman to live by herself."

"You could stay with me."

"*Nein*, it's not the same. You're a widow, but since I've never been married, Daed forbids it."

"*Jah*, he's right. I'm going to miss you."

Hannah nodded. She took her glass to the sink and started washing dishes.

After Hannah went home, Sarah drank the rest of her lemonade and sat in silence. What was she going to do without Hannah?

Gott, *You have taken everything from me. What do I do now?*

* * *

Morning came too soon after her restless sleep. Sarah pushed herself out of bed, hurried to get dressed, hitched King and trotted him all the way to the Millers' farm for the preaching service. Preaching was at the Millers' farm this month. Hannah usually rode with her but when she stopped at her house, Hannah claimed she had a headache and stayed home.

Sarah sat on a bench and prayed, hoping it'd ease the pain of losing Hannah and her folks. She closed her eyes and swallowed the glumness in her throat.

Her life had changed directions again. *Move on. Don't cling to the past. Look forward to the future.* She took a deep breath and blew it out.

But she knew she needed to trust Him.

Bishop Yoder's preaching about losing a kindred soul, as well as his testimony, touched her heart and filled it with peace. She was still reeling from the inspiration when they read the banns and announced Ezra Smith and Hannah Ropp's names. They were getting married…in two weeks!

I can't believe Hannah didn't confide in me. Courting was usually a secret, but she was Hannah's best friend.

After church, Sarah ate her meal in a hurry and

hitched her buggy. She urged King into a fast trot, jingling the harness rings and sending his hooves pounding on the roadway. Her heart thumped her ribs the whole way to Hannah's *haus*.

John Ropp was standing in the barnyard when she arrived. Preparation had already begun for the wedding in two weeks. "You must have heard the good news." He smiled as he held King's reins so Sarah could step down from the buggy. "I'll put King in the barn to cool off. He looks hot." John patted the animal to calm him.

She ran into the Ropp *haus* and knocked on Hannah's door.

She heard Hannah giggle. "Come in."

"Headache, huh?" She ran over and smothered her friend with a hug. "Congratulations. You kept the secret from me, of all people."

"I wanted it to be a surprise. You should have guessed by the big garden Daed put in." A tear ran down Hannah's cheek. She snatched a hankerchief from the bureau drawer and blotted both eyes.

"I'm so happy for you, Hannah. Are you moving to Missouri?"

"*Nein.* Ezra and I are staying here. Mamm and Daed won't move until after the wedding."

"That's an answer to my prayer. I can hardly believe it."

"I'm not going to Missouri, but Ezra's farm is

at least thirty minutes away, so we probably won't get to visit often. Since you're staying in Kalona, I can stop by when I'm in town. But I'm really going to miss Mamm." She sighed.

Sarah put a hand on Hannah's back. "You can call her from the phone shed and write letters. Besides, you'll be so busy with his *kinner,* you won't have time to get lonely or bored."

"*Jah*, you're right." Hannah sucked in a breath. "I'm so excited. Let's go downstairs on the table and start planning the wedding with Mamm."

They tore down the stairs and ran to the kitchen like they did when they were *yung*. "Mamm, sit and help us plan the wedding."

The three of them worked out the details and made a list of things to do: need postcards for invitations, scrub floors, get benches and tables, polish silverware, borrow dishes, make up dinner and supper menus. And clean the *haus* from top to bottom.

This listing went on and on until the afternoon melted into evening. "I need to get home and get some sleep. I'll see you tomorrow."

On the way home, a giddy notion slipped into Sarah's head. She smiled and pretended for a moment that it was her and Caleb's wedding. When she finally got to bed, sleep did not come easy.

The next day, Sarah returned to Hannah's *haus*

to help with preparations. "What's next on your to-do list?"

Edna frowned. "Are you sure you want to do it?"

Sarah looked at the list. "It looks like I've just volunteered to wash the borrowed dishes and polish the silverware." She drew in a deep breath. "I better get started."

Edna patted her on the back. "It will be a big help. I have so many things to do, and John is frantic. Hannah is in her bedroom, working on her wedding dress. That leaves me to do everything else. My cousins won't be by until this afternoon to help." Edna sighed and went off into the other room.

A knock on the door startled Sarah. She glanced around. "Edna?"

No answer. She dried her hands on a towel and hurried to the front door.

It was Caleb and Mary. "*Hullo!* What are you doing here?"

Caleb smiled. "We came to offer our assistance."

"Mary, why don't you go upstairs? Hannah would *liebe* to see you. She's in her room, first door on the right. Caleb, John is frantic with work. He'll *welkum* your assistance."

"Jacob is already helping him. He's picking up sticks in the yard."

"*Gut.*"

"It was the least I could do after the incident at the fair when I thought Ezra and…well, you know."

She nodded. "Do you remember what you told me once?"

He shook his head.

"In order for a relationship to work, trust has to come first."

Caleb blushed as he smiled at Sarah. "*Jah*, now I remember."

As he walked beside her back into the house, Sarah's cheeks flushed, as well. All these wedding preparations had a way of turning one's mind to thoughts of marriage and weddings.

She wondered if she and Caleb would ever stand before the bishop together, but Caleb had never mentioned the idea of marriage. A prudent woman would walk away from this relationship and chalk it under nothing more than friendship. But what more romantic place was there than a wedding to give Caleb a nudge?

As Ezra and Hannah said their vows in Pennsylvania Dutch, butterflies fluttered in Sarah's stomach. When the bishop said a blessing and pronounced them *ehemann* and *frau*, Sarah's throat clogged. Hannah, her childhood friend, getting married was like another chapter in her life folded and tucked away. She would miss her friend.

The meal after the wedding consisted of roast duck, turkey and chicken with all the trimmings. When the chairs at the tables scattered all around the house were full, the bishop gave the signal for silent prayer. Then everyone waited for the first clink of silverware against a plate before beginning.

Sarah glanced at the cakes she and Mary had made and placed on the *Eck*, the bridal table. Mary had done a *wunderbaar* job; lemon cake was Hannah's favorite.

Sarah laughed as she sat next to Hannah at the table and squeezed her hand. "Frau Smith, you are radiant."

Hannah laughed. "I can hardly believe I'm married. I'm too excited to eat."

When it was time for the bride and groom to visit with their guests, Sarah wove her way through the crowd, looking for Caleb. Many of their customers from Amish Sweet Delights and The Cookie Box had come.

With all the people milling around, spotting him was hard. A couple of times, she caught a glimpse of Bishop Yoder, but headed quickly in a different direction. Except for one time when he called from a distance and told her he wanted to introduce her to Elmer Plank. *Nein*. She was through allowing the bishop to matchmake for her. She wouldn't hurt Caleb again.

Hannah's wedding gave Sarah a chance to talk to so many people in the community she hadn't seen in a while. Later she caught sight of Mary carrying dishes into the *haus*, and hurried to catch up with her. "Mary, have you seen your *daed*?"

"He was talking to Kathryn Miller under a tree in the backyard." Mary shrugged.

Sarah wandered through the yard, talking to people as she went. When she rounded the corner of the *haus*, she spotted Caleb standing under the chestnut tree with Kathryn. Widow Miller laughed loudly at something Caleb said and touched his arm. He smiled back at her.

She waited a moment in the shadows. A sliver of distrust swept over her… Guilt prickled up her back. Trust was the very thing Caleb said that two people had to have. Relationships were built on trust.

Turning around, she headed back to the kitchen to help with the dishes. Mary stood at the sink, stacks of dishes on both sides. Sarah stepped between Mary and one of Hannah's relatives. "I'll help out so you won't be here all night."

The relative looked delighted at Sarah's offer.

Mary picked up a plate to dry. "I'm glad Hannah's staying in our community. She will probably miss her *mamm*. I still miss mine, but I like to talk to Hannah." Her voice choked with emotion. "It was a beautiful wedding. Hannah looked so in *liebe*."

Sarah wrapped an arm around Mary's shoulders and hugged her. Surprisingly, she put her arm around Sarah's waist and hugged back. She knew Mary didn't have many female relatives, and she could tell it would have been another loss for her if Hannah had moved.

After grabbing a dish towel, Sarah dried the next plate in the drain rack.

A short while later the door opened and Caleb, with Jacob in tow, sauntered over. "Mary, it's getting late. Are you ready to go home?"

She turned toward Sarah. "Anything else I need to do?"

"*Nein. Danki* for your help and baking the cake."

"Sarah, I'll pick you up Sunday so you can attend Sunday school with us." Caleb's eyes twinkled, and he gave a smile that made her knees turn to mush.

"*Jah*. Who could refuse a smile like that?" She threw the dish towel over her shoulder, perched her hands on her hips and raised a brow. She was falling for him, all right. Remorse pricked the back of her neck for having a hesitant heart when she saw him with Kathryn.

He hadn't said he loved her. Yet. But wasn't that what she was reading on his face? Was he only looking for companionship?

She still had so many questions. And not enough answers.

Chapter Nineteen

Sarah opened her Bible to Jeremiah 29, and searched for the answer to why *Gott* took away everything she loved. Would He take Caleb away, too? When she came to the eleventh verse, she read it over and over. *"For I know the thoughts that I think toward you, saith the Lord, thoughts of peace, and not evil, to give you an expected end."*

She had always believed that *Gott* had taken Samuel and her bakery from her, and had closed her womb. *Nein.* He wouldn't harm her.

Jeremiah 29:11 is saying that *Gott* cannot keep us from suffering, but He will share our burden and carry us through. He was there all the time. He'd given her Samuel's love. Hannah's friendship. It all boiled down to the fact that she had to trust Him.

A knock on the door startled her.

She glanced at the clock. *Ach*, Caleb. She slid her Bible and study guide into her bag and hurried to answer the door. "I'm ready. I'll just grab my things." She slipped her cape and bonnet on and locked the door behind her.

She settled into the buggy, beside Caleb. "I enjoy attending Sunday school and Bible study with your church group. Old Order still believes only the church should interpret scripture, so they don't encourage group study. It's probably one of the biggest differences in our Orders. That, and the use of mechanical conveniences. Yet Old Order has a better youth retention rate than New Order. Did you know that, Caleb?"

"*Jah*. It's a concern for us. Many think the youth leaving our Order is because we believe in evangelizing and going out into the community. It teaches the youth too much about the outside world and not about staying within *our* community. I worry about Mary and Jacob leaving the faith after they go through their *rumschpringe*." Caleb glanced her way with worry lining his eyes.

"Do you think you will ever change back to Old Order?" She hadn't meant to blurt it out, but she had to know.

"I need the use of the tractor and other mechanical devices, like the rototiller, bulk milk tank, and mechanical milker for farming." His face flushed red. "I can't change."

There it was. Her heart plunged to the floor. Her church and her family would shun her if she left the Old Order to marry Caleb. Neither of them was willing to give in. She drew a deep breath, met his gaze with a weak smile and reached over to pat his arm. "Jacob and Mary will stick with the faith—I'm sure of it. They'd miss you too much."

He took her hand and squeezed it lightly before letting go, but a cloud of uneasiness hung between them. Sarah shifted her weight and gazed out the window at the harvested fields. They looked as bare and bleak as her hope for a marriage to Caleb. "Since Hannah is married, I was thinking about moving to Iowa City and opening a regular bakery." A plan she'd just now hatched since chances seemed slim she'd be marrying Caleb.

Snowball held a steady pace as the buggy bounced over ruts in the country road. Finally, Caleb's voice cut through the stillness. "Tomorrow I'll get a driver and take you to Iowa City to start your search."

"You're a *gut* friend to do that for me."

"You helped Mary can tomatoes, and that's hard work in the heat. I'll be glad to repay the favor."

She gripped her bag. *He thinks he needs to repay the favor. That's all.*

What was the point of them spending time together if marriage wasn't in their future?

Caleb rose early and dressed. He'd slept restlessly, at best, with dreams of Sarah constantly waking him. Iowa City was eighteen miles away. By horse and buggy, that was almost an hour. He'd have to rent a car and driver whenever he wanted to see her.

He took a calming breath, rubbed a hand over his chest and tried to ease the ache. What was he going to do without Sarah? He could ask her to marry him and not wait for Mary and Sarah to work out their differences. Surely Mary would come to accept Sarah. The question was…could he convince Sarah to change to New Order?

The driver picked him and Jacob up on time, then headed for Sarah's *haus*. She was waiting at the door with her bag, spiraled notebook and pencil in hand, and an optimistic smile on her face. How could he convince Sarah to stay in Kalona? He stepped out of the car and held the door while she slid in, next to Jacob. He hopped back in front next to the driver.

"Jacob, I'm glad you are coming along while I look for a bakery. I value your opinion very much." She patted his arm.

"Why do you have to move to Iowa City? I

want you to stay in Kalona and run The Cookie Box so I can visit you."

"Jacob. Sarah has lost Hannah and must make other arrangements." Caleb glared at his *sohn*.

Sarah handed a slip of paper with an address to the driver. "*Hullo.* I'm Sarah. We have an appointment with a real estate agent to look at a couple of empty shops."

He took the paper and nodded. "Eddie. Have you there in a few minutes, ma'am."

Soon they were walking around an old, dilapidated shop. She looked in closets, cupboards, nooks and crannies. She glanced at the ceiling and knocked on the walls.

Caleb took a deep breath. It would take her a year to fix this place up. He could help but he had farm work. Doing this much alone was impossible.

Sarah glanced at the real estate agent, Marge, who waved her arms around. "It's old but it has a charm to it."

Caleb snorted.

Sarah shook her head and Marge motioned toward the door. "The next building might be more what you had in mind."

Caleb cringed at the idea of Sarah staying alone in Iowa City. At the next spot, he glanced around at the expensive cupboards and counters and whistled. "What do you think of this place, Sarah?"

"It's a lot of money. I'd have to hire help in order to make enough to support myself and pay the rent. I'd have to charge a lot more than I did in Kalona." Discouragement hovered in her voice.

At the third place, he took her hand and helped her up the steps. Her palm was cold and clammy. He looked around the shop and whistled. "A fancy shop, *jah*?"

She nodded. Her forehead furrowed, and her eyes clouded with worry.

Jacob rubbed his hand over the brown marble counter. He blew out a big puff of air, trying to whistle. "*Jah*, this is *gut* and looks like an *Englisch* bakery. Can I come and stay with you? I'll work hard on Saturday."

"Jacob!" Caleb tossed him a cross face.

"I'd rather stay with Sarah." Jacob pouted.

Caleb regretted his outburst. He knew the *bu* was scared of losing Sarah. He was, too.

Sarah caught Jacob's hand and held it while they exited the building. Caleb wrapped his arm around her shoulder. "It's time we stopped for lunch. Let's go to a nice restaurant. We can rest and talk about some of the shops you wrote under the Maybe column on your notepad."

"That sounds *gut*." She said goodbye to Marge and told her she'd be in touch.

"Eddie, would you mind taking us to A Little Bit Country restaurant on Melrose Avenue? We'd like you to join us."

"No, thanks. I'll come back and pick you up in an hour. The missus will have a delicious dinner waiting for me, so I don't want to spoil my appetite."

The hostess seated them at a table by the window and handed them menus.

Sarah opened her menu. "Caleb, this is expensive."

"It's my treat. Order whatever you like."

She took a deep breath and studied the selection for several minutes. She laid it down on the wine-colored tablecloth and lightly rubbed her hand across the rich linen. "Nice."

"I'm glad you like it. Relax. Take that worried look off your face. They'll think we can't afford to pay."

She laughed. "I'll try."

Their waitress brought them water, took their orders and quietly stole away.

"You didn't find anything you're serious about today?" He could tell she was thinking about her answer.

"I have money saved, but it'll take a lot to set up the shop. It's expensive here. I'd have to charge a lot more for the baked goods in order to pay for the rent. I'd also have to hire several people to help me. So it's definitely something I'm going to have to think about before I make a decision."

"Wait until spring," Caleb offered, trying to make it sound sensible.

"If I waited until spring and needed your help, you'd be out working in the fields."

"Don't worry. I promise you, we'll figure something out. But take your time. This isn't a decision to be made lightly." He watched as she moved her silverware around and took a sip from her water glass. Her brow furrowed. *Jah*, she was mulling it over. He hoped she came to the same conclusion that he did.

The waitress brought their food to the table. "I'll stop back later. Enjoy."

Sarah took a bite of her sandwich. "This turkey on the homemade bread is delicious. It has tomato and melted cheese and some kind of sauce. How's yours?"

"Mine is *gut*. Jacob, is your sandwich tasty?"

"Nein."

Caleb read the hurt in the *bu*'s eyes. "Jacob, Sarah has to run her business, and there is already one bakery in Kalona."

"Jah. But I want her to stay. She can come live with us."

"Nein, Jacob. She cannot do that."

Sarah quickly changed the subject. "Even if I don't get a shop selected today, it was worth the trip to Iowa City just to eat here. This restaurant is charming."

The server stopped at the table with a water pitcher and refilled their glasses. "How are your meals?"

Sarah's face glowed as though she were a *kind* visiting a restaurant for the first time. "*Wunderbaar.* Could I see a dessert menu, please?"

"Sorry, the pastry chef quit and the new one hasn't started yet."

"Oh, that's too bad."

"Haven't I seen you before?" The waitress looked at Sarah with a scrutinizing eye. She glanced at her clothes, then at Caleb. "You look familiar. Wait a minute. Do you run that Amish Sweet Delights bakery in Kalona?"

"*Jah*, I'm Sarah Gingerich. I did operate the bakery, but my *bruder* sold it."

"Oh, too bad. Your baked goods were wonderful." She handed the water pitcher to another server before stacking their empty dishes on a tray. "Nice to see you again. Just in town, enjoying the day?"

"I'm looking at shops in Iowa City and thinking about opening a bakery here."

"Hope you find one. It'd be nice having your bakery close by."

Caleb paid the check and helped Sarah slide her chair back. He glared at Jacob and his sandwich with only a nibble out of it. "Since you didn't eat your lunch, don't ask for a treat later." He gestured to his *sohn* to lead the way to the door.

"Excuse me." A well-dressed man hurried toward them. "Are you Sarah Gingerich?"

She stopped and faced the speaker. *"Jah."*

"I'm Kenneth Gardner. I'm the restaurant manager. I've visited your bakery before. You make delicious desserts."

"Danki."

"My pastry chef quit and my new one doesn't start for four weeks. I was wondering if you'd be able to bake desserts for me for a few weeks. Either here at the restaurant, or if you bake them at your bakery, we could make arrangements to have someone pick them up."

"I live in Kalona."

"One of our workers is from Kalona, so he could pick them up on his way to work. We'd advertise them as Amish desserts. We'll call it a special for the holidays. Since we're located in the heart of the Amish community, our customers may like the change."

"I could maybe do it for a few weeks. What kind of desserts?"

Caleb could hear the excitement in her voice. He took a step closer to the door.

"Pies, apple crisps, brownies, cookies—that type of thing. Let's step over here and talk about it further. I'll introduce you to Mike Matthews. He'll be the one to pick up the baked goods."

When they left the restaurant, Caleb flashed Sarah a smile. "Congratulations."

Sarah held up a hand. "I'm still shaking. I can't believe it. It's only for a few weeks, but it made me feel *gut* they even asked. And with this arrangement, the baked goods are preordered. I'll need an organizer put in the pantry in my kitchen and some more shelves."

"Write out what you need. I'll pick it up and be over tomorrow to get started."

"I might do what you suggested, Caleb. Just stay in Kalona for the winter, keep The Cookie Box and work on my cookbook."

Caleb forced a grin from his face. It was all music to his ears.

Sarah stood back and surveyed the organizer and extra shelving Caleb had installed in her house. "*Wunderbaar.* I don't know how I'll repay all the work you do for me."

"No repayment needed. You're a friend, Sarah. I enjoy helping you."

His words struck her like a cold snowball to the cheek. Was he trying to tell her that's all she meant to him? A friend. She forced a weak smile. "I'd like to make you supper to repay you."

"Another time. I want to get home to Mary and

Jacob." He gave a wave as he closed the door behind him.

She unpacked her saucepans from the storage box, washed and hung them. The high-ceilinged room echoed as her shoes clomped across the wooden flooring. It reminded her of how empty the house was without Caleb's presence. She needed to stay busy and forget about such things.

She clutched her first order from A Little Bit Country to her chest. Working for a five-star restaurant was a *gut* move, even if the job was only temporary. If she opened a bakery in Iowa City, maybe they'd continue to give her business. That meant she needed to make them some very tasty desserts.

After pulling her supplies from the pantry, she started on the brownies. When those were in the oven, she stirred up the cookie dough and baked five dozen chocolate chip and oatmeal raisin cookies. Next she started a batch of yeast rolls rising. They didn't ask for the cinnamon rolls, but she'd throw them in as a *danki* for the orders and give them a sample. While those were set aside to rise, she made a chocolate cake and the apple crisp, then finished making the rolls.

Sarah packed all the desserts into boxes, which took until the wee hours of the morning. She set the baked goods on the table, sat in the rocker and waited for Mike Matthews, the man from the restaurant, to stop by.

The knock at her front door startled Sarah out of her snooze. She jumped off the rocker and found Mike on her front porch. "Mornin', Mike. They're all ready for you."

"Morning, Sarah. Fall asleep, didya?"

"*Jah.* Since I closed the other bakery, I'm not used to working late and getting up in the middle of the night."

He laughed. "See you in a couple of days."

She locked the door behind him and headed to bed for a little more sleep.

Two days later, she had a new order from the restaurant. Mr. Gardner's order included a note. *Thanks for the cinnamon rolls you included free last time. Our brunch crowd raved about them.*

It paid off. He'd ordered five dozen cinnamon rolls. For the next order, she'd include two dozen sample dinner rolls and a free apple strudel. This order would take all night. At times like this, she wished Hannah was still around to help her, but Hannah was happily taking care of her *ehemann* and his *kinner*.

When Mike knocked the next day at 5:00 a.m., he handed her a slip of paper. "Chef Randy loved your desserts. He asked me to give you the name and address of his publisher to get your cookbook published. You still have time to get them printed to sell for Christmas. Randy's *Little Bit Country Cookbook* sells out over the holidays in the restaurant gift shop."

"*Danki*, Mike." Sarah laid the note on the table and helped Mike carry the boxes to the car.

The next day when Mike dropped off the order, there was a note stapled to it. Besides their usual order, they'd added three apple strudels. She grinned. Free samples were always her best advertisement.

Sarah had hoped Caleb would stop by so she could share her exciting news with him. Each time horses' hooves clopped on the pavement in front of her *haus*, she peeked outside. But each time, the buggy passed by.

Why hadn't he come by?

With his stomach signaling time for dinner, Caleb finished his chores and headed to the house. He opened the kitchen door to black smoke engulfing the room. He ran to the stove, grabbed a pot holder and pulled the unattended frying pan off the burner.

Jacob ran into the kitchen. "What's that smell?" He wrinkled his nose and made a face.

"Looks like our dinner. Where's Mary?"

"She went outside."

"How long has she been gone?"

"I don't know. A long time. She told me to play in my room."

Mary slammed the back door and turned to face her *daed*. "*Ach*. Smells like burnt roast. I had the roast simmering in water. Guess it must have boiled dry."

"You can't leave food on the stove with a lit burner and go out of the *haus*. You know better than that, Mary." Caleb raised his voice. "Where were you?"

"Sorry. I just stepped outside for a breath of cool air. The kitchen was hot." Her tone was unapologetic.

"It takes a while for meat to boil dry. Why were you outside?"

"Talking to some girls. I walked with them down to the creek and back."

"That is a mile away. The meat is burnt and Jacob was here by himself."

"I'll fry some hamburgers." She slowed her words, but her voice shook.

"You'll do no such thing. Go clean up that mess, and Jacob and I will fix sandwiches."

After Mary and Jacob went to bed, Caleb sat and stared into the dark living room. He missed Sarah every second of every day. He rubbed his forearms. Even they ached for her.

Caleb glanced at the clock on the oak mantel as it chimed midnight. *Jah*. Past time for bed. He pulled change out of his pocket, dropped it into a glass dish next to the clock and listened to it clink on the bottom.

He rubbed his hand across the mantel and looked at his fingers, then at the trail they left in the dust.

He wouldn't blame Mary if she decided to take an afternoon and read a book or visit with a friend. She deserved the time off. He was gone the whole day. She worked as hard as any woman, cooking and cleaning all day. But a dusty *haus* was puzzling, and out of character for her.

He whisked a finger across the sideboard, the end tables and the wooden chairs. They were all dusty. He scratched his head. Recently, meals had been lighter and simpler than usual. Now when she cooked a beef roast, she went outside while it cooked. She had burned food before, but he'd thought she was busy with the cleaning and laundry.

He stroked his beard. Something was going on with Mary. He could ask Jacob, but he attended school most of the day.

Was she interested in a *bu*? Maybe.

He'd never seen her talking to any *bu* at church. At least not that he'd noticed, but he didn't watch her every second. Should he ask her? Would she tell him what was going on if he did?

Sarah would know what to do.

Chapter Twenty

On Friday Sarah had the last order for A Little Bit Country restaurant all ready when she pulled the door open.

A weird sadness suddenly rushed through her. She enjoyed Mike's chatter, and seeing him every week. But that wasn't it. *Nein.* She enjoyed working for the restaurant. It gave her a feeling of pride, but if the bishop knew that, he would make her confess. It wasn't a conceited pride. The recipes for the desserts she'd sold the restaurant belonged to her, and not her *daed*. She'd always worked under her *daed*'s shadow. It was the reason she'd written the cookbook—to prove to herself she could do it.

"Mornin', Mike. Your order's ready. Has your new pastry chef started?"

"No. Not yet." He smiled and pulled a sealed envelope out of his pocket and handed it to Sarah.

"I'm supposed to wait for an answer. I'll load the car while you decide on a reply."

Ach. Maybe they wanted her to keep baking a few more weeks. She unfolded the paper and read. Then sat and read it again. Excitement surged through her. "Tell Mr. Gardner I'll be in to see him tomorrow." Her throat tightened. It was a *wunderbaar* opportunity.

She closed the door behind Mike and stumbled to a chair. This was something she'd never expected. Pastry chef. Their new chef had found another job and wasn't coming. They were offering the job to her. She needed a job to support herself. If she bought a shop, it might be months, maybe years before she'd break even.

This was perfect...or was it?

She'd have to hire a driver to take her the eighteen miles to work every day. Maybe she could ride with Mike on the days he worked. Or she could rent an apartment in Iowa City. It was a *wunderbaar* opportunity, but could she leave Kalona? Leave Caleb and his family? She'd hardly ever get to see them.

Tears streamed down her cheeks and sobs heaved her shoulders.

Caleb knocked on the door and waited. He hunched over against the raw wind and pulled his coat tightly around his neck. As soon as the door opened, the warm air hit his face.

"Come in out of the cold." Sarah waved toward the table. "Have a seat. I have hot coffee to warm your bones."

"*Nein.* Let's not give the neighbors something to talk about. Why don't you come with me to Lazy Susan's café?"

Sarah slipped into her black bonnet and heavy cape, locked her door and hurried to his buggy.

When comfortably seated at the restaurant, she ordered coffee and one of Susan's cinnamon rolls. "I might as well try the competition."

Caleb smiled at her selection and ordered the same.

The waitress nodded. "Just take a minute."

"What brings you to town today? An errand?" Sarah asked. "It's a cold day to be out and about."

"I wanted to talk to you about Mary." He stopped abruptly at the presence of the server. She set the coffee and rolls down.

Caleb took a bite of roll. "They're not as *gut* as yours." He raised his brow. "You're the best roll maker I know."

"*Danki.* I appreciate your loyalty."

Caleb stirred cream into his coffee, the spoon clinking against the glass cup a little too much. He noticed her eyes darting from his cup to meet his gaze.

"Is there something wrong, Caleb?" She sat back in the chair.

"I wanted to ask you something about Mary."

"Mary?" A tone of surprise tinged her voice.

"When you helped her can tomatoes this summer, did she say anything about a special *bu* she might have liked?"

"A *bu*?" She gasped. "Why do you ask that?"

"Mary has been acting strangely lately."

"What do you mean?" She took a sip of coffee, looking over the rim of the cup at him.

"Clothes aren't getting washed when they need it. The living room is dusty. Last night's supper was burnt, and she left Jacob alone in the house."

"Mary doesn't say much to me about anything, unfortunately."

"You must have talked about something during canning."

"We talked and said it would only be two years and she would be attending singings. I asked if she was excited about that, and she said *jah*."

"So, she was talking about boys."

"Don't jump to conclusions. I asked if she liked a special *bu*. She said *nein*."

"But that was a few months ago. She could like one now," he insisted.

"Have you talked to her?"

"*Nein*." He picked up a spoon and stirred his coffee again.

"Tell her what you've noticed and ask if there is a problem." Sarah tapped the table with her fingertips. "Go home. Sit her down and talk with her."

"Maybe I'll give her a little longer and try to keep a better eye on her."

Sarah raised a brow. "She's a young woman. Maybe she bought a romance novel and lost track of time reading. Without a woman around to give her advice, maybe she's searching for answers on how to act around *buwe*."

He leaned back, took a deep breath and exhaled. "You're probably right. She's normally a responsible girl. I know it must be hard when she doesn't have an older sister or a *mamm* to tell her things."

"Mary is sensible. Just talk to her." Sarah reached across the table and patted his arm. "And now that we have settled your problem, I have some good news to tell you. A Little Bit Country restaurant has offered me the job of pastry chef, and I'm going to take it."

His heart nearly stopped. He drew in a deep breath. His body wouldn't move. It was as if he were a frozen snowman. Her penetrating gaze thawed his shock. "Did I hear right? They offered you a job as a pastry chef."

"Jah." She gave a nervous laugh. "I can start

whenever I want. I was hoping you could take me to Iowa City to find an apartment, and help me move."

He wanted to shout *nein!* from the top of a barn. But how could he? If he demanded she stay, what could he offer her? Neither of them wanted to change to the other's Order. Tears threatened his vision, but he lowered his chin and blinked them back. His heart was ripping in two. He swiped a hand through his beard. "*Jah.* I can do that. I'll miss you."

His chest hurt so badly, he could hardly speak. She was like his right hand. *Nein.* Not just his hand. Sarah was part of his soul, and she was ripping it apart.

"Have you started to pack?" he stammered.

She nodded.

"I'll take you home and come back tomorrow morning at eight with a car and driver to take you to Iowa City." He laid his money on the table and stood.

She chattered about her new job all the way back to her *haus*. He dropped her off and headed Snowball home in a slow trot that allowed him to decide how to tell Jacob the news. It would crush Jacob's heart to lose Sarah from his life. The knot tightened in Caleb's abdomen as he tried to decide how to come to terms with Sarah's decision.

He worried Mary was sneaking out with some *bu*. He didn't want to lose her. Not yet.

Instead, he was losing Sarah.

The Amish taxi pulled into Sarah's driveway on time. She grabbed her bag and darted out the door, adrenaline and excitement fueling her feet.

They arrived at the restaurant at 9:00 a.m. The old Victorian building was going to be a *wunderbaar* place to work. At least, it helped ease her aching heart to tell herself that. Remembering where Mr. Gardner's office was from her last visit, she started in that direction.

"I'll wait at a table," Caleb called as he headed that way.

Mr. Gardner's secretary escorted Sarah into his office and closed the door. He motioned toward the furniture. "Sarah, I'm so glad you decided to join us."

"*Gut* mornin'. *Jah*, I'm ready." She sat but held her back straight so it hardly touched the red brocade chair. Her hands rubbed the rich texture of the fabric. It looked too fancy to sit on.

He reclined behind his mahogany desk in his high-backed brown leather chair. "We had many compliments on your desserts. When the pastry chef decided he didn't want to move from Florida to Iowa, you were the first person that came to mind."

"*Danki*, Mr. Gardner." Her heart fluttered from the flattery.

After they settled on her salary, and her days off, they discussed her starting date. "I'm looking for an apartment in Iowa City, and as soon as I find one, I'll move. Meanwhile, can I work from home and have Mike pick the baked goods up? I'm hoping it won't take more than two or three weeks."

"That'll work." He stood. "I'll introduce you to Chef Randy. He'll show you around the kitchen. He has heard of you through the Amish tourism books and has tried your desserts. He's a big fan of yours and is very excited to work with you."

"*Danki,* Mr. Gardner. I'm excited about this opportunity."

But if she were truly excited about the job, then why didn't her heart agree?

Caleb was hoping it would take several visits to Iowa City before Sarah found an apartment. Instead, she found the perfect apartment about a mile from the restaurant. It was small but move-in ready. She'd have to store most of her furniture, but it wouldn't require much care if she worked late hours.

"I'll let you know when I'm packed. Could you ask Ezra's friend with the truck if he could help me move?"

"Of course."

"I have another favor. Could you keep King and my buggy at your place for a while? At least until I see how this job and living in Iowa City are going to work out? Mary can use the buggy, and King is a *wunderbaar*, gentle horse."

"Glad to do it. You'll need to come out and say goodbye to the *kinner* before you leave town."

"I'll do that when I drive the buggy out."

The memories of the *gut* times he'd had with Sarah came flooding back. His heart felt swollen and ready to burst out of his chest at the thought of never seeing her again. At least not often. He forced the lump in his throat away.

Her warm smile stayed with him all the way home. When he entered the *haus*, he checked on his *kinner*. They were both in their rooms. He sat in his rocker for a long while, staring around the room at Martha's Bible, her fabric scraps in the corner and her quilts.

He went to the pantry and pulled out the cardboard box he saved to carry Mary's canned goods and jellies to market. He packed all of Martha's things from around the house into the box and set it in storage.

As he climbed the stairs to his bedroom, several steps squeaked under his weight. He'd been so busy helping Sarah lately, he'd neglected his own home's repairs.

Caleb sighed. With her gone, he'd have plenty of time on his hands for repairs. But his heart wouldn't be the same without Sarah in his life.

Chapter Twenty-One

Her hands shaking, Sarah slowly slipped the harness on King and tightened the girth. "This is the last time I'll hitch you, at least for a while. I have to work and take care of myself." She rubbed his ears and mane, then glanced into his large brown eyes. He shook his head, snorted as if he understood and nervously paced the ground.

She slipped her handkerchief out of her bag, wiped away tears and blew her nose. "We best get on our way to Caleb's farm."

She climbed into the buggy and tapped the reins against King's back. The harness pulled taut as the buggy jerked to a start.

Sarah glanced up. Gott, *I can't believe that I'm on a totally different road for my life. I have no idea where You're leading me, but I'm going to miss Caleb, Jacob and Mary.* She gasped for a breath of air, then continued. *The agony is rip-*

ping my heart in two, but I must trust that You have placed me on the right path.

When King pulled into the driveway, Jacob and Caleb ran out of the *haus* to meet her. Mary followed at a slower pace. Sarah smiled as Mary approached. Slow was better than not at all. Caleb helped her down. Jacob hugged her.

"Mary made us hot tea and rolls to share as your last sit-down with us. I'll unhitch King and put him in the barn."

"I'm going to miss you. Don't go," Jacob sobbed.

"Jacob, we talked about this." Caleb's stern face tossed him a warning.

"Please don't go!"

"Jacob, help me unhitch King while the women go inside."

Sarah caught the jerk in Mary's head as she looked at her *daed*. He'd called her a woman.

Mary led the way into the *haus*. "Living in Iowa City will be *wunderbaar*. Are you excited?" She banged the teakettle as she poured the hot water into the teapot, then set the basket of loose tea in the pot to steep.

"*Jah*, excited and nervous. I'll have no close Plain friends there. You can use King and my buggy."

"Really? *Danki*. Can I visit you sometime and stay a few days?"

"*Jah*, that would be fine, if your *daed* says you can."

Caleb and Jacob banged the door as they entered. They took their coats and hats off and placed them on hooks.

Jacob sat on a chair, his head down, lips poked out in a pout.

Mary set the plate of rolls she'd made on the table and poured the tea. "It's ready."

Sarah sat next to Jacob, but he still wasn't in a talking mood. She took one of the rolls and munched a corner. "Mmm. This is delicious."

"*Danki*. Caramel-pecan, Mamm's favorite."

"Your *mamm* must have been a very *gut* baker."

"*Jah*. She had many talents. So do you, Sarah. You're going to work at a fancy restaurant as a pastry chef."

"Think you'll like living in the city?" Jacob asked between bites and sniffles.

"Maybe, but I'll miss the country, and all of you, very much."

Sarah finished her tea and brushed a crumb from her skirt. She glanced at the clock and stood. "My driver should be here any minute. I don't want to make him wait."

"I'll go check." Caleb walked to the window and looked out. "He's here. I could go with and see that you make it okay."

"*Nein*, Caleb. That would be harder for me. The

driver is taking me back to Kalona to get the last of my luggage and run a couple of errands before we leave for Iowa City."

They walked out to the SUV, and each one gave her a hug. "*Danki* for your *liebe* and friendship, and for your *wunderbaar* cooking, Mary." She climbed into the Ford and buckled her seat belt.

As the vehicle pulled away, she waved. Sarah gazed out the far window of the vehicle so Caleb wouldn't see her face. As soon as they were out of the driveway, she pulled out her handkerchief and wiped the tears from her cheeks.

Caleb's chest tightened. *You're a fool, Caleb Brenneman. You should have asked her to marry you. Now it's too late. She's excited about her new job as a pastry chef. You can't burst her dream.*

He walked to the barn and cleaned his workbench and tools. He trudged back to the *haus* and closed the door against the cold, brisk wind. Maybe a hot cup of coffee would soothe the knot in his throat.

Caleb hung his hat and coat on a peg and took a whiff of an unpleasant odor that permeated the air. "Mary, you burned dinner again, didn't you?"

She turned away from the stove. "Sorry, Daed. I only stepped outside for a minute."

"What's gotten into you, Mary?"

"Nothing."

"Daed, can we go see Sarah?" Jacob pouted.

"Sit and eat. We'll talk about it later."

"There are only chicken and vegetables to eat. Mary burned the potatoes."

They clasped hands and Caleb said the prayer. He examined the potatoes. A little scorched where they touched the pan, but still eatable.

"Yuck. These potatoes taste terrible. They make my tongue taste awful." Jacob gulped a drink of water.

"Why don't we go see Sarah in Iowa City tomorrow?" Mary took a bite of potatoes and ate them. She wrinkled her nose and shook her face at Jacob. "They don't taste so bad. You're such a *boppli*."

"Didn't think you liked Sarah. You just want to go to Iowa City." Caleb pointed his fork at Mary.

"I want to see Sarah and eat one of her cookies," Jacob chimed in.

"I want to see where she lives," Mary added.

Caleb dropped his fork, the metal clinking as it hit the glass plate. "You've never cared about Sarah. Why the change of heart?"

"That's not true. She made me a birthday cake and helped me can vegetables all summer. She showed me how to cook several dishes. Why wouldn't I like her?"

"Why are you saying that, Mary, when you know you gave her the cold shoulder after she took your *mamm*'s leftover scraps to make a book cover?"

"I'm over that. I had wanted to make a memento to remember Mamm. But I probably would never have gotten it done, and the one Sarah made looks *gut*."

Caleb pushed his chair back, scraping the legs on the floor, and threw his arms in the air. "All this time you liked Sarah and never said anything?"

"I certainly don't like Widow Miller. Sarah is much better for a *mamm* than Kathryn. I can't believe you didn't ask Sarah to marry you."

"*Jah*, Daed. Marry Sarah. Then she can come live with us," Jacob squealed.

Caleb turned to Mary. "You like her now?"

"I like her and I can tolerate her a lot better than Kathryn. Kathryn has set her *kapp* for you. The way she bats her lashes when you're around." Mary rolled her eyes.

"What does 'set her *kapp*' mean, Daed?" Jacob raised puzzled eyes.

"Never mind, Jacob."

"Why hasn't the laundry been getting done, or the cleaning? Why is the food burnt now half the time?"

"I'm tired of doing all the housework. Soon I'll

get married and have to do everything by myself. I want a life first. I want to go skating with my friends. I want to have fun."

"Mary, you shouldn't say things like that. Should she, Daed?" Jacob shook his head.

"Jacob, please. Mary and I are talking."

Caleb sat back and rubbed a hand across his forehead. It was hard work for a woman to manage a whole household, let alone a fourteen-year-old *mädel*. He should've hired help.

"I can't see my friends—there's no time. A few of us have been going down to the frozen creek and skating."

"And you leave Jacob here all by himself? What if he got hurt?"

"Exactly. If I go do anything, I feel guilty because I took a little time away from all this work." She waved her arms around. "It was nice when Sarah was here, helping me. I know I shouldn't have gotten mad at her over those scraps of material. Mamm wouldn't have liked my behavior."

Mary raised her gaze to Caleb. "You let Sarah go. I thought you loved her. Go after her, Daed."

He headed outside. He needed some cold air to clear his mind. All this time, Mary had played games with him instead of being honest.

Nein. That wasn't the truth. She was truly hurt at first when Sarah took the scraps. Apparently when Sarah helped her and taught her like a *mamm*, she forgave Sarah. Then *Gott* healed her grieving heart.

He'd made a mess of things.

He heard the kitchen door close behind him and two sets of feet walking across the porch.

"Daed, you need your coat. Are we going to get Sarah?" Mary asked.

"Jah. Get ready. You, too, Jacob." Caleb ran into the *haus,* grabbed his coat and hat, and threw them on while he raced to the barn.

"Hurry, Daed. Hurry." Mary yelled. "Before she leaves her *haus* in Kalona."

Caleb hitched Snowball to the buggy while the horse paced the ground in place as if he sensed the urgency. Caleb motioned and the *kinner* jumped in behind him. He tapped the reins on Snowball's back. The buggy lurched ahead as the horse set the wheels in motion.

When they turned onto the roadway, Snowball increased his gait to a full trot toward Kalona. The three miles to town seemed more like twenty to Caleb as he reined the horse to a stop. Sarah's yard and driveway were empty.

"Wait here." Caleb stepped down, hurried to the door and knocked.

No answer.

The man on the porch next door waved Caleb over. "She left a few minutes ago for Iowa City. If you hurry, you might be able to catch up with them. I heard her say she needed to stop at the bank, and she had to turn in the house key."

"*Danki* for your help."

Caleb headed toward Route 218 at the edge of town to wait for the SUV.

Sarah already missed Caleb and the *kinner* so much, her heart was about to burst. After she settled in to her apartment, she'd bury herself in work at the restaurant until she'd adjusted to life without the Brennemans.

Caleb was obviously not ready to remarry, and she understood that. Martha had only been gone not quite two years. Yet it was difficult seeing him when he didn't want a relationship, only a friend, a companion.

When the SUV slowed, she glanced out the window and noticed a buggy sitting along the side of the road with Caleb, Jacob and Mary waving for them to stop. She tried to slow her racing heart. She'd probably forgotten something at their *haus*, or they just wanted to wish her well again. She stepped out of the SUV.

Jacob tore out ahead of his *daed* and Mary, skidding to a halt in front of her. He threw his arms around her in a hug and sobbed.

Sarah rubbed his back and whispered. "I'll miss you, too, Jacob."

"Don't you want to be my *mamm*?"

She froze.

What in the world was this *bu* talking about? How could she ever face Caleb? The heat burned on her cheeks.

Caleb and Mary hurried over and stood a few feet away from her and Jacob. Sarah glanced up. She drew a ragged breath and noticed the broad smiles on their faces. She patted Jacob's back as he continued to hug her.

Caleb took a step closer. Sarah's gaze met his.

Caleb's lips twitched and his eyes sparkled like precious stones. His eyes captured and held hers. "*Jah*, sorry, Sarah, but I imagine there are worse proposals than that."

Did he say what she thought he'd said? Did Caleb Brenneman just propose to her?

Caleb stepped forward and patted Jacob. "It's my turn. Let me give her a hug, too."

Jacob stepped back and rubbed his shirtsleeve over his eyes and down his cheeks.

Caleb wrapped his arms around Sarah and gave her a tender kiss. When he pulled away, he locked eyes with her and whispered, "*Ich liebe dich.* I love you, Sarah."

"*Ich liebe dich*, Caleb Brenneman." She looked over at Mary's smiling face. "And I loved the way the whole family asked. I wouldn't have wanted it any differently. My heart is overflowing with *liebe* for you all. *Jah*, I'll marry you…for sure and for certain."

Cars were driving by with windows down and people clapping. Some held cell phones out the windows, taking pictures.

"Oh, no!" Mary laughed. "This is going to be all over the internet." Mary hurried and put her iPhone in her pocket, but not before Sarah witnessed the act. Their gaze met and Sarah gave Mary a wink.

Sarah stepped back. "I need to call Mr. Gardner and tell him I won't be taking the pastry chef job after all."

Caleb grinned. "Maybe you can bake for him until he hires a new chef."

Sarah nodded.

"Mary, I almost forgot." Sarah darted to the SUV, hurried back and handed the book to Mary. "I forgot to give you this earlier." Sarah wrapped an arm around Mary's shoulders.

Mary stared at Sarah for a few seconds and glanced at the book in her hands, *Baking the Amish Way* by Sarah Gingerich. She turned the front cover over and spotted a note written on the inside.

Sarah whispered the words to Mary. "To my darling girl, Mary. I treasure you in a very special way. May God always bless you and guide your footsteps. May your days always bloom with joy, like the flowers of the garden. And may you always cook and bake with love. Yours in a very special way, Sarah."

Mary raised tear-filled eyes to Sarah. *"Danki."* She wrapped her arms around Sarah and gave her a kiss on the cheek.

Sarah returned the hug and kissed the top of Mary's head.

"They're my *mamm* and *daed*'s recipes, and some I developed myself. Your copy is the very first one off the press. I made sure of that."

Sarah gestured toward the crowd gathering around them. "We made quite a spectacle. If folks didn't know what the Amish people were like, they got their eyes and ears full today."

"Jah, they did." Caleb sighed. "That's the thing with us Plain folk. We like to keep life exciting in a simple kind of way."

Sarah feasted her eyes on Caleb and pulled him close once again. "I'm never going to let you three get out of my sight."

"Does that mean you are willing to give up the bakery and come be a farmer's wife?"

"After I left your farm and before I even got back to Kalona, I discovered it wasn't the bakery that mattered to me. It was you, Jacob and Mary. The thing I want most in life—to be part of your family."

Epilogue

"Sarah."

Ach. She stopped and cringed. *The bishop.* Only fifty feet from her buggy. She turned and waited for him to catch up to her.

"Bishop Yoder, I'm married now. You certainly don't want to introduce me to another widower, do you?"

He laughed. "But every time I introduced a widower to you, he ended up married—to someone else. The only exception was Elmer Plank."

"*Jah.* Elmer is a really nice man." She nodded. "I'm working on introducing him to someone. We'll see how it turns out."

"Ah, *gut.* Then I can turn the matchmaker hat over to you. What I really wanted to ask was how you managed to convince your *ehemann* to join our church. I didn't think Caleb Brenneman would ever come back to the Old Order."

"Old Order has a better youth retention rate, and we want to keep the *kinner* close. Again, thank you, Bishop, for marrying Caleb and me last Thursday. We really appreciate you clearing your schedule."

"It's almost Christmas. You should be with your loved ones for the holidays." He turned to leave, then glanced over his shoulder. "I wasn't taking any chances on getting you two married." He winked at her. "*Gut* day, Sarah."

As he walked away, she chuckled. "You're an old softy, Bishop."

"Don't tell anyone that, or I'll deny it." He raised his hand in the air and waved.

Sarah hurried to the buggy, grabbed her *ehemann*'s hand and snuggled close to him. "Sorry you had to wait."

Caleb turned to her as he gave the reins a tap on Snowball's back. "What did the bishop want?"

"Oh, just to see how I liked married life."

"I hope you told him it is *wunderbaar*." Caleb smiled.

Sarah slipped her hand around his elbow and squeezed. "Of course, *liebling*."

"And you don't miss being a pastry chef?"

Sarah hesitated. "Maybe a little bit, but I'd rather be with my family."

The snow began to fall as Caleb turned the

buggy into the drive. Sarah shivered. "It's cold. Who wants hot cocoa?"

Everyone said, "Me," at the same time.

"Cookies and cocoa in fifteen minutes." Sarah hurried into the house and shook the snow off her cape. "Mary, we'll need to start making Christmas cookies tomorrow."

"Have you talked to Daed yet about us opening a bakery?" She pulled out a saucepan and grabbed the milk.

"Not yet. I'm waiting for the right time." She glanced over at Mary as they worked side by side.

Mary set cups, plates and spoons on the table. "I'll fetch the cookies," she called out as she headed to the pantry.

Out of the corner of her eye, Sarah caught Caleb sneaking up behind her. He planted a big kiss on her cheek.

"I *liebe* you." His breath tickled her face.

"I *liebe* you, too." She turned around, wrapped her arms around his neck and pulled him close for a tender kiss.

"I'm going to like being married. And to think, I almost lost you."

"*Nein.* That was never going to happen. You just needed a little nudge." Sarah glanced around and noticed Mary had disappeared from the room.

"What? You had this planned all the time?" His eyes widened.

Sarah smiled. "Come on, everyone, the cocoa is hot."

Jacob pulled out his chair and sat. "Mamm, I'm ready for my snack now."

Sarah smiled at her new name—Mamm.

When Mary stood behind her chair, Sarah noticed she held something behind her back. Mary brought her hand in front and held up the book cover that Sarah had made out of Martha's quilt scraps. Mary folded the book cover back to display Sarah's cookbook.

"Now I'll always have both of my *mamms* right here, at my fingertips and in my heart, always."

Sarah ran and gave her a hug. "*Danki.* That is the best Christmas present you could have given me." Tears clouded her eyes and rolled down her cheeks.

Gott had been with her on this journey all along to give her what she needed. For sure and for certain, how could she ever have doubted Him?

* * * * *

If you enjoyed The Amish Baker,
*look for these other emotionally gripping
and wonderful Amish stories*

The Amish Bachelor's Baby
by Jo Ann Brown
The Promised Amish Bride
by Marta Perry
Her Amish Child
by Lenora Worth

Available now from Love Inspired!

Find more great reads at
www.LoveInspired.com

Dear Reader,

I grew up on a farm in northern Illinois, not far from Amish country. When we would drive to town, I'd see Amish buggies and horses. That form of transportation looked like fun, so I asked my dad why we didn't have a horse and buggy. To my disappointment, he explained it was part of their religion to give up modern devices. From then on, the Amish have intrigued me.

Now I live seventy-six miles from Kalona, Iowa, and visit there often. The Amish started to move to Iowa in 1846 to live a more secluded lifestyle. The different groups—including the Old Order, New Order and Beachy Amish—have settled in seven Iowa counties.

In *The Amish Baker*, Sarah Gingerich, who is Old Order, and Caleb Brenneman, who belongs to the New Order, struggle with what their church *Ordnung* requires and what their hearts want. Like Sarah and Caleb, sometimes we might feel as though God has left our side. That is, until we discover that the impossible can come true and God is faithful and has never left us.

I love to hear from readers. Tell me what you enjoyed or what inspired you. Email me at

Bast.Marie@yahoo.com, visit me at mariebast.blogspot.com and facebook.com/marie.bast, or follow me on Twitter.

Blessings,
Marie E. Bast

Get 4 FREE REWARDS!

We'll send you 2 FREE Books plus 2 FREE Mystery Gifts.

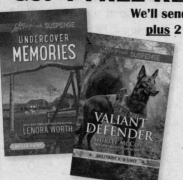

Love Inspired® Suspense books feature Christian characters facing challenges to their faith... and lives.

FREE Value Over $20

YES! Please send me 2 FREE Love Inspired® Suspense novels and my 2 FREE mystery gifts (gifts are worth about $10 retail). After receiving them, if I don't wish to receive any more books, I can return the shipping statement marked "cancel." If I don't cancel, I will receive 4 brand-new novels every month and be billed just $5.24 each for the regular-print edition or $5.74 each for the larger-print edition in the U.S., or $5.74 each for the regular-print edition or $6.24 each for the larger-print edition in Canada. That's a savings of at least 13% off the cover price. It's quite a bargain! Shipping and handling is just 50¢ per book in the U.S. and 75¢ per book in Canada.* I understand that accepting the 2 free books and gifts places me under no obligation to buy anything. I can always return a shipment and cancel at any time. The free books and gifts are mine to keep no matter what I decide.

Choose one: ☐ **Love Inspired® Suspense**
Regular-Print
(153/353 IDN GMY5)

☐ **Love Inspired® Suspense**
Larger-Print
(107/307 IDN GMY5)

Name (please print)

Address   Apt. #

City   State/Province   Zip/Postal Code

Mail to the Reader Service:
IN U.S.A.: P.O. Box 1341, Buffalo, NY 14240-8531
IN CANADA: P.O. Box 603, Fort Erie, Ontario L2A 5X3

Want to try 2 free books from another series! Call 1-800-873-8635 or visit www.ReaderService.com.

Get 4 FREE REWARDS!

We'll send you 2 FREE Books plus 2 FREE Mystery Gifts.

Harlequin® Heartwarming™ Larger-Print books feature traditional values of home, family, community and—most of all—love.

FREE Value Over **$20**
